The Fifth Di...
March 2025

Features

Short Stories

Flash Fiction

*

THE STAFF OF THE FIFTH DI...:

EDITOR: Tyree Campbell
WEBMASTER: H David Blalock
COVER DESIGNERS: Laura Givens; Marcia A. Borell

Cover art "Walkabout" by Laura Givens
Cover design by Laura Givens

Vol. V, No.4   March 2025
The Fifth Di... was published three times a year on the 1st day of April, August, and December in the United States of America by Hiraeth Publishing, P.O. Box 1248, Tularosa, NM, 88352.

This is the last issue of The Fifth Di... to be released by Hiraeth Publishing

A Little Help, Please

In the world of the small indie press we fight a never-ending battle for attention to our work, as writers and in publishing. Here's an example: big publishers [you know who they are] have gobs of $$$ that they can devote to advertising and marketing.   Here at Hiraeth Publishing, our advertising budget consists of the deposits for whatever soda bottles and aluminum cans we can find alongside the highways. Anti-littering laws make our task even more difficult . . . ☺

That's where YOU come in. YOU are our best promoter. YOU are the one who can tell others about us. Just send 'em to our website, tell them about our store. That's all. Just that.

Of course, we don't mind if you talk us up. We're pretty good, you know. We have some award-winning and award-nominated writers and artists, plus other voices well-deserving to be heard [not everyone wins awards, right?] but our publications are read-worthy nevertheless.

That number once again is:

www.hiraethsffh.com

Friend us on Facebook at Hiraeth Publishing
Follow us on Twitter at @HiraethPublish1

Pevely Keiser in:
THE IPHAJEAN LARK

Five hundred years into the future, Pevely Keiser is the capo of the criminal organization called Temmen. Temmen runs itself, for the most part, with only a few nudges from Pevely to keep people in line. Lately she has two things on her mind. She wants to do something good and useful with the funds that accrue to the gang. And she wants a companion or two to help her...and perhaps to share her bed, for she well knows it's lonely at the top.

In the process of training her two new assistants (and possible companions) Pevely comes across a young woman being chased. Taking her on board, Pevely soon learns of a devastating conspiracy that threatens the Confederation with totalitarian rule. The key to the solution lies in the hands of one of her employees, but is it the right key? Only the corporate hierarch who leads the conspiracy knows for sure. And he is the father of the woman Pevely rescued.

https://www.hiraethsffh.com/product-page/iphajean-lark-by-tyree-campbell

Hadullen Island
Stephen Kramer Avitabile

It was the first island I ever saw up close, pure and beautiful, so simply magnificent. I was so young, but I knew I was seeing something that bordered on perfection. Our boat bounced around on the waves as we passed by what they called Hadullen Island.

There were settlers on the island. Some were curious to make a home there. Some were curious of the island's natural resources. Especially of the resource unique to all islands, Pink Rock.

The palm trees swayed in the slight breeze like they were waving to me from afar. The beaches were a welcome beige and the greenery on the island was lush. On the shore closest to us, I saw a female. I couldn't tell her age. Was she a kid like me? Was she a teenager? Was she an adult? I didn't know but she had a pretty face and a simple, happy smile.

The man running the boat dropped another Blue Rock into the engine and as it was ground up the engine roared back to life. He told us there were many more islands to see and we motored away. He was right. I saw many more islands that day. But none compared to that first island. Hadullen Island.

A few years later I managed to work my way onto another boat tour to see the islands. I was still a kid, so it was difficult to get passage onto the boats. I had to save up a lot of Green Rocks from doing odd jobs around the village just to convince the captain to let me on. He agreed. And we jetted through the waters.

We saw many islands; some were new to me. Some I remember seeing from my first tour. And eventually we saw Hadullen Island. It sat in the water in all its original beauty. Completely unchanged. And on the shore, there stood that same beautiful female. I still could not tell her age. It would stand to reason that she aged a few years as a few years had passed but it was impossible to tell. She looked exactly the same.

I asked the captain if we could head to the shores and explore Hadullen Island. He looked at me like I had traded in all my Green Rocks for Red Rocks and cackled with laughter. He pointed out all the settlers on the island. I didn't see them at first but then they became clear.

"Too much competition." He said. "Those shores are already claimed. You'll have to hope the settlers leave someday."

He tossed a Blue Rock into the engine and we jetted away. The female on the shore locked her eyes on our boat for a moment. I watched her and considered waving but then she turned away and walked inland. The palm trees didn't wave to me in the wind. Perhaps there wasn't enough wind. Perhaps they didn't care to wave. Perhaps they were just palm trees.

We saw a few more islands on our tour. I remember seeing two more that I found to be pretty. One was small, full of rocks. It didn't look too welcoming. One was large, the beaches glowed a teal color and there were maroon trees sprouting mysterious, large maroon fruit. That island had a lot going on. Almost too much.

The captain said it was his favorite island to see. I disagreed. It was pretty. But it lacked a natural beauty I wanted. It lacked what Hadullen Island had.

I was finally old enough to drive a boat myself. I had to do more odd jobs and collect more Green Rocks. I needed to pay for lessons and for the certificate, and of course, to rent a boat. I worked myself hard. I was 15, the minimum age to drive a boat. Not many 15-year-olds were seen driving boats around here. Any that you did see were wealthy. And then there was me.

I set out into the waters and went straight for Hadullen Island. I had heard just months before that the settlers had deserted the island. I hoped this was still true. The waters were choppy, and I bounced around in the tiny boat so much that my head felt like it would pop off my neck.

I saw the shore of Hadullen Island and I saw no one there. I rode my boat right up onto the beach and hopped out. I rushed up onto those beautiful beige beaches. A sweet aroma hit me, pulling me inland. Perhaps vanilla? Baked goods? I followed the scent up the beaches and towards the tree line. The forest was not so thick. It provided shade once underneath the canopy, but ovals of sun burst through the branches above providing spotlights of sun all around the beautiful dirt floor. I saw occasional red flowers blooming on the trees and the sweet smells were growing stronger.

And then I saw her. That same female. She stood in the middle of the forest. I could make out her face much better. Warm and friendly brown eyes, smooth and radiant skin, large blushing cheeks, and a chin that almost came to a point. But I still could not tell her age. But I got the distinct feeling she was the same age as me. She smiled at me, keeping her lips pressed together. The sweet aroma was so strong now. It satiated a hunger in my stomach. That was, until I saw a few settlers exit from behind some of the thicker trees. They nodded to me but were more interested in rooting around in the dirt.

The female, actually, the girl who was my age, I became quite sure of it at that moment, she kept smiling but her smile became sad. Her youthful skin glistened under a spotlight of sun and her innocent eyes stayed on me. When I looked back to the settlers, she looked at them too. More of them were searching for the island's natural resources in the dirt. The Pink Rock. The Pink Rock which I had heard so much about but had never seen myself.

I retreated from the forest, back to the beach, back onto my boat, and I drove off. I passed by a few other islands on my way home. Some were pretty. One struck me as beautiful, Crasnor Island. I wasn't sure if it seemed beautiful to me because of the fact that it was deserted, and Hadullen Island was not. But perhaps I'd have to find beauty elsewhere.

It took me five months before I had enough Green Rocks to rent a boat again. This time I took it right to Crasnor Island. I had remembered where I encountered it. When I arrived, it was still deserted. I walked the beaches; the sand was so hot it seared right through the bottoms of my cheap shoes. The sand was an eggshell color and the trees in the distance were mint green with thin, brown-yellow trunks that were so smooth they looked like they were professionally gift wrapped.

My legs carried me into the forest, I had no say in the matter. The forest held a humid atmosphere inside and it smelled like oranges and lemons. My legs pulled me closer to the scent until I came across a woman... another whose age was difficult to determine. She was all ages at once, but up close, she looked mostly like she was in her 30's.

She watched me with curiosity. I greeted her and she simply nodded. I dropped to my knees on the dirt floor, and I began to dig. The forest was quiet besides the occasional chirps of exotic birds. I dug several divots in the dirt and came up empty. I moved to a new position and dug several new holes. On my 11th or 12th hole, my fingers scraped against something solid. Pink shone through the brown dirt. I dug around the object and pulled out a large Pink Rock.

As I pulled the Pink Rock out of the dirt it felt attached to roots of the earth. I yanked and yanked until I completely freed it. The Pink Rock softened in my hands... transitioning from the hardness of a rock to the softness of a head of lettuce.

The woman continued to watch me, and her lips pressed together tightly. I was perplexed at what happened with the Pink Rock. But I broke off a piece and handed it to her. She gladly accepted and waltzed into the forest. I took my find back to my boat, tossed a Blue Rock into the engine, and jetted back home.

I took the Pink Rock to a market I had heard about from the old men who frequented the cafe where I bought croissants, muffins, and coffees. I heard them mention many times that this market was fair. An appraiser looked over my Pink Rock. He examined it closely. He told me it was a good size, but he frowned when he saw how soft it had gotten. He told me the harder the better but that this was still a great find for my first one.

He asked what I wanted to do with the Pink Rock. I asked him what my options were. I admitted that I had no idea. He said some men trade them for Green Rocks and Blue Rocks, but they are usually sour, old men who do not smile. He told me other men trade them for Orange Rocks, but they are the men who drift through life without emotion in their eyes. He didn't peg me for any of those types of men.

I agreed.

The appraiser then told me that most men will have him, or any appraiser, turn the Pink Rock into a tea or a soup to consume. He said he did this for a fee of a few Green Rocks. He scanned the market with his eyes and then he leaned in close to me in a hushed tone.

"But you can do this yourself at home. You don't need me to do it. Would you like to know how?"

I told him I would like to know how. He explained to me quickly and quietly and sent me off on my way and didn't ask for anything in return.

The information was strange. The way the appraiser handled it was strange. The world was strange... and I didn't quite understand it. But I was young. Maybe that would change as I got older.

I went home and made a tea of the Pink Rock. I followed the appraiser's instructions exactly and the tea turned out just as he told me it would. I sipped the tea as I sat in my bed. It was delicious, a slight hint of orange and lemon. The tea made me feel fantastic. It was a feeling that lasted all night. My brain felt as if it had opened up. I wondered if I would've felt better if the Pink Rock hadn't softened so much when I pulled it from the dirt. That night I had the best sleep I had had of my life... to that point.

It was another four months before I had accumulated enough Green Rock to rent another boat. I went back to Crasnor Island and there were still no settlers there. I headed into the forest and the woman emerged again. She told me she was happy to see me. I asked what she did with the Pink Rock, and she said she made a soup from it and that she enjoyed it. I asked her if she ever pulled the Pink Rocks from the island herself. She told me that was impossible. I asked why and she told me it was because she was the island.

I suddenly became aware how quiet it was in the forest... besides the occasional birds. There was no one else on the island... at all. Just me and the woman... the woman who claimed she wasn't a woman, rather, she was the island.

I dug around for another Pink Rock and eventually found one. It wasn't as large as the last one, but it was attached to ropy, vine-like objects in the dirt, so I had to tug until it was free. As I freed it, the Pink Rock softened once more. Not as soft as the last one, this one felt like a week-old zucchini in my hand. I offered some to the woman, but when I looked up, she had vanished. And she had just been there! There was a slight rustling in the trees and the air whipped around... orange and lemon scents so strong... and then they faded completely.

I went home and made myself a soup of the Pink Rock this time. It was delicious once again. I felt fantastic all night... once again. The taste and the feel were slightly better. I wondered if it was because I made a soup this time or if the Pink Rock wasn't quite as soft this time. I fell asleep with that on my mind, bouncing back and forth between the possibilities.

When I was 16, I went on another excursion to Crasnor Island but when I arrived I saw settlers were there, searching for Pink Rocks. I suppose that was to be expected, so I continued through the choppy waters. I surveyed the area and found another island that I had seen before.

The island smelled very minty. The aroma was sharp and overwhelming. I dug around for Pink Rocks. I dug so many holes. I kept coming up short. Piles and piles of dirt surrounded me. And then I found one, but when I pulled it from the earth, it crumbled in my hand. Several soft pink pieces in my hand. I was shattered... as shattered as the Pink Rock. I took it home with me and attempted to make a soup.

It was a sharp, minty soup which would've served me better as a tea, but in any event, it was tasty. Not delicious. It made me feel good. Not fantastic. I'd need to explore more islands.

Over the next couple of years, I began working more and more, gathering more Green Rocks. I was able to rent a boat for several excursions. Each time I tried a new island and had varying degrees of success. Every time I pulled a Pink Rock from the dirt it softened, but not to such degrees each time. Every tea and every soup I made was tasty and better than any old tea or soup, but some were much better than others.

I found one with spicy, chocolate scents circling the forest. They were such different scents and the tea that the Pink Rock made was delectable, so I went back there a second time. I left with another Pink Rock. I tossed a Blue Rock in the engine of the boat and roared away.

I remembered that Hadullen Island was near here, so I took a detour to pass by... see how it was. As I approached, I could smell those wonderful smells again. I had forgotten how intoxicating they were. I couldn't believe they were reaching out to me in the waters... but wonderful baked goods and vanilla aromas lingered in my nose. I moved closer to the island and approached... and there was the girl... on the shore. All the way on the edge... right by the water. I figured this girl was also the island... as every girl of every island that I met had told me the same thing. But I had never seen one so close to the water.

She spotted me and waved me over. The island was deserted. It was just her. I looked in my bag, but I had no more Blue Rocks. I had thrown the last one in... I wouldn't have enough to get back to shore if I stopped. I yelled out to her and tried to tell her this. I didn't know how much of it she understood. I didn't know how much she could even hear over the roar of the waves and the static spray of ocean smashing into the jagged rocks.

I veered away from Hadullen Island and headed back. I made my Pink Rock tea... and it was good... but for some reason it had lost a bit of its allure. The spicy chocolate indulged me last time. But this time, all I could think about was vanilla.

In my quest to gather enough Green Rocks to make my way back to Hadullen Island now that it was finally deserted, I took on a lot of work. Whatever I could find. One day I was high up on a ladder working on a roof when I fell off and broke my leg.

Couldn't walk or work for a while. Time was just passing me by. I hated it. As soon as I was able to work again, I kicked it into overdrive. I slept less and worked more. I stacked up Green Rocks and finally had enough to rent a boat and jet out to Hadullen Island. I reached the shore, and no one was on the beach. I ran through the sand, my sights locked on the forest. The closer I got, the stronger those lovely vanilla smells grew, but the louder some foreign noise grew. I couldn't make out what it was over all the other island sounds.

Until I pushed past the thickest of trees and found settlers digging through the forest floor. Beaten out once again.

I felt defeated. I didn't go to any other islands. I went home. I didn't want to work anymore. But I told myself that I needed to. And I started work the very next day. And the day after that. And after that. I don't recall if I took any days off. The only days I didn't work were the days I couldn't find work. I refused to stop. Not until I had enough Green Rocks.

Not enough to rent a boat.

Enough to buy a boat.

I finally reached that milestone. I bought a simple boat, and I left this side of the mainland. I drove clear to the opposite side, bordering the warmer waters, and I built a new home for myself there. I had my own home and my own boat. I continued with the same odd jobs on this other side of the mainland. I worked for Green Rocks and sometimes Blue Rocks. I took my boat out into the waters, and I scanned all the islands. I never touched the shores of any of them until I was sure I had seen them all and examined them all.

I eventually started to visit the islands, but I hardly had any luck with Pink Rocks. So many settlers found islands before me. So many visits to islands and coming up empty handed. And so many Pink Rocks I took home that were small or that crumbled in my hands.

My boat was the one shining positive. I went where I wanted when I wanted.

And one day, I wanted to go back and visit my original home. It had been a few years since I'd been on the old side of the mainland. I packed up plenty of Blue Rocks and I traveled around the long way, taking in the sights. It was scenic and wonderful. But I knew in the back of my mind, I had another reason for this. Even if I wouldn't admit it in the forefront of my brain.

The route took me past Hadullen Island. I made sure to give it a long glance. And there she was. On the beach. Toes so close to touching the water. Waving me in.

So, I allowed her petite hands to beckon me in. My

boat felt as if it was pulled in by those dainty fingers. The beach had changed over the years. It was raised. I wouldn't be able to drive my boat onto it. But I could park it just next to the beach. I hopped out of my boat onto the beach and tied it up. It began to sink in the water, and I wasn't sure why. The girl told me that the waters at the shore were heavy and had a pull. The solution was to keep the boat running. So, I did. I loaded a couple Blue Rocks in the engine and the boat floated once more. The girl brought me into the forest, and we were surrounded by extravagant beauties. The lush green trees featured warming red flowers at every turn. The deeper we went into the forest, the more of these lovely red flowers there were, and the more vanilla aromas surrounded us.

She brought me to a place in the forest and pointed to a soft patch of dirt. She told me to dig. I did. I discovered a large Pink Rock. I wrapped my fingers around it and was ready to tug but she placed her palms on the backs of my hands and grasped them firmly. She held my hands still. She was the island, but I could feel the distinct feelings of warm fingers and warm skin on me. I could feel soft leaves brush my fingers as well. She told me to remove the Pink Rock gently. I told her it would be tangled. She said she knew this but to trust her. So, I listened. I gently pulled the Pink Rock from the dirt with her hands guiding mine.

The roots were attached, and they extended from the dirt, clinging on. But I kept pulling slowly at the request of the girl... the island. As I lifted the Pink Rock higher, slowly, the roots untangled and fell off the Pink Rock, landing with soft thuds in the dirt.

I was astounded. The Pink Rock retained all of its hardness. It was a large one, an amazing specimen. The girl told me to follow her. We walked deeper into the forest. More of the red flowers were popping up all around us. And then the girl led me to a cave with a wide opening. She strolled inside the opening and went deep into the cave. I followed her and we reached a space covered in the red flowers. She must have been picking them for months. The cave floor was lined in these pure red flowers. Their petals looked and felt of satin. There was one corner of the cave that had an extravagant pile of the red flowers, bunched together like a bed. She sat at the edge, and by her feet was a fire that was dying. She brought the fire back to life and prepared the necessary material to make Pink Rock tea.

I sat next to her on the flowers. We were surrounded by bright apple-red colors, like we were the only two non-red entities and surrounded by warmth on all sides.

We drank the tea together and it was the best thing my tongue ever tasted. She told me to stay, and she would show me how to pick the Pink Rocks. She said the island, her, she was littered with them. I could stay here as long as I wanted. And we could drink tea every night.

I agreed. I ran out to the boat and tossed in a few more Blue Rocks so it would float throughout the night and then returned to the cave. We slept in the sea of red. Me and the island. On the island.

The next few days went on like this. We went around and found Pink Rocks. She showed me the ways to remove them in certain situations. It was a skill. Not every Pink Rock was in the same situation. Each one required a different method of being removed. She showed me the ways. I continually loaded Blue Rocks into the engine of my boat so it would remain afloat. We drank tea, we indulged in soup, we had the best time.

And we slept on the red flower petals.

I felt safe. I felt the warmth no matter how cold the nights got.

One morning we exited the cave, and I said I would go add Blue Rocks into my boat's engine. She said she'd wander the forest and pick red flower petals. I raced off, I didn't want to waste a single second. I stopped at a river to catch my breath and cool my face off. I checked my bag. I had enough Blue Rocks for another day or two. I would have to let her know that I'd need to momentarily leave to retrieve more Blue Rocks. I would tell her when I returned.

I splashed more cool water on my face from the river. It ran down my forehead and cheeks and to the back of my neck. It was sweet, cool relief from the hot sun above. I closed my eyes and relaxed, breathing slowly, savoring my lovely situation. I heard a soft splash. And another. Another. I opened my eyes to see that I hadn't closed my bag tightly enough and all my Blue Rocks were tumbling out of my bag into the river!

I yanked my bag back up but not quickly enough! All of my Blue Rocks had fallen out of my bag. I jumped into the river and followed my Blue Rocks as they were swept away in the quick current. The river deepened and I fought through it. The currents pulled at my legs, and I struggled to keep my balance. I did my best to run, to follow the Blue Rocks, but they kept gaining separation. The river pulled at my legs harder. I slipped and fell, splashing down into the water. The river began to pull me along. I clamored to my feet and looked ahead.

A waterfall.

The current was too strong. My Blue Rocks were too far ahead of me. And the waterfall was too tall, I wouldn't survive a drop like that. I pulled myself out of the water as best I could, collapsing on the riverbank just as all my Blue Rocks went over the edge of the waterfall.

I followed the riverbank all the way up to the cliff that the waterfall tumbled over. I peered down and saw jagged rocks lining the pond at the bottom. Blue smoke billowed off the jagged rocks... not the sign I wanted. All my Blue Rocks were lost. Every single one of them. I wanted to race to her, to find her, but I couldn't waste any time. My boat's engine was already low, if it ran out it would sink, and I wouldn't be able to retrieve it. I had no choice, I had to make my way to the boat.

As it was, I made it to the boat, and I could hear the roar of the engine softening. I didn't have much time. I hopped in and drove off. I looked back to the island in hopes I would see her, and I could shout something out to let her know I would return. But I didn't see her. But she was the island. So, I called out to her anyway. In hopes she would hear me. The palm trees didn't wave. Nothing moved on the island.

And the scent of vanilla faded.

I headed to my old village and my boat barely was able to putter up to the shore before the engine died. I docked my boat, leapt from it, and instantly began to ask around for Blue Rocks. Everyone I asked said they didn't have any. I ran from person to person, market to market, no one had Blue Rocks. The sad reality was that I had plenty saved up at home, on the opposite side of the mainland.

I eventually found the appraiser; the original one I went to years ago. He remembered me. I asked him about Blue Rocks, and he said he didn't have any and that there was a drought. There hadn't been any on this side of the mainland in months. They were all on the other side and it was difficult to get a hold of any over here.

That was all I needed to hear. I turned on my heel and ran. Away from the water... as painful as it was... I was distancing myself from Hadullen Island. But I needed to reach the other side of the mainland. I needed to reach some Blue Rocks. So, I ran inland.

It was no short distance and I wasn't aware of anyone who had crossed the entire mainland on foot. But it had to be done. The first day I covered much ground. I found a shady spot near some large trees, foraged for mushrooms and plants, and fell asleep. I awoke with the sun and began running inland again. I couldn't waste any time.

That second day was scorching hot. I kept ducking for cover under trees. I had to pace myself to keep from fainting. There were large stretches of land with no cover, so I was forced to take cover and rest and wait long whiles. I didn't cover as much ground as I would've liked. By nightfall, I found another place to eat and sleep. But I awoke in the night, thankfully, and I began running again while the moon was high in the sky. I could cover more ground before it got too hot.

I passed by the mountains before the sun arose and approached the forest soon after. The terrain was more difficult to cross inside the forest, but I took that path with another hot sun in the sky. It was easier with the shade provided. I reached the edge of the forest by nightfall and slept there. The next morning, I took off once again, and I finally began to find pockets of civilization. Each person I came across I asked about Blue Rocks. No one had any.

I asked 11 people that first day. I slept in the shade of a large hut that night and I kept running inland the next morning. I came across many more people that next day. Each one I asked for Blue Rocks. 27 more people to tell me no. And the next day, 13 more people to tell me no. But I was almost home. I had almost crossed the entire mainland. At this point, my place was right around an upcoming bend. I came across more people but didn't bother to ask them anything, I would just go right to my home.

I burst through the door, wheezing, doubled over. My body felt like it might give, but I mustered my strength. Whatever I had, I summoned it. I still needed to get my hands on my Blue Rocks. I found my stash and collected them all. I noticed I had some Pink Rock soup still left over from a different island. I considered having some to nourish myself... but I didn't want soup from another island. So, I left with my Blue Rocks.

I stopped at the market for a quick meal to regain my strength. I met someone who had a boat and was traveling to the other side of the mainland. He said he would give me a lift for some of my Blue Rocks. I would still have plenty leftover, so I agreed.

He brought me back to the other side of the mainland and dropped me off at my boat while the sun was still in the sky... but it was sinking. I wasted no time. Blue Rocks in my boat's engine, it roared to life, and I was off!

I prayed I would make it to Hadullen Island as quickly as possible. I prayed my explanation would suffice; I did a lot of praying. So much that I almost distracted myself from driving the boat. Massive waves came from nowhere and nearly capsized me. I corrected the boat and focused my mind... focused my sights ahead.

The boat raced. My mind raced. And then I saw Hadullen Island. The sun was sinking more but there was still light in the darkening blue and orange sky.

I left my boat in the water next to the shore, Blue Rocks in the engine keeping it afloat. I shut my bag tightly and I ran for the forest. The scent of vanilla was faint, but it was there. The forest was dark... not as dark as I would've expected. That was lucky for me, I could see where I was headed, identify obstacles on the first floor, and avoid falling flat on my face.

I entered a slight clearing in the forest and there she was. Standing next to a fire. A fire built by another settler. I tried to explain... explain where I was... explain where I had gone... but my mouth didn't know what words to bring forth on my tongue. My jaw bounced around like it was broken.

The settler looked up and saw me, but he didn't say anything. I didn't say anything. She, the island, didn't say anything. So, I left. I left the island. I went back to the mainland.

Back to my original home. I stayed in an abandoned hut that night. The next morning, I jetted back to my home on the other side of the mainland. A home that felt empty and deafeningly quiet.

I never set foot on Hadullen Island ever again. I explored other islands. New islands. I took what I learned from Hadullen Island with me. How to forage for the Pink Rocks. The gentle touch. The knowledge that each case is vastly different, no two situations the same. I learned so much and I put it to good use. Not that I ever wanted to use that knowledge anywhere else. I thought I had found a home... a true place to live... on Hadullen Island.

It shaped me. It made me who I am today. And to be frank, I am proud of who I am today.

But I still pass by Hadullen Island occasionally. Usually at night when no one can see me. Sometimes while the sun is still up. The shores remain beautiful. The palm trees still wave. I catch glimpses of those perfect red flowers from afar. I swear, nothing else in life is as red as those flowers. I looked. I hoped to find materials to make a bed sheet the same color. But I never found anything so pure red.

But sometimes I see it flash in front of my eyes, usually when I allow myself to indulge in a sweet vanilla treat. Something I do quite often, actually. I'm only human, after all. It was only an island, after all. But not *only* an island.

The Spark
By Stephen C. Curro

Katrina grew up in a frigid world ruled by a tyrant. By day, she works as a mechanic. At night, she becomes the Ace, the King's personal assassin. She's not proud of her job, but she's accepted that it's the way things are. At least she has her boyfriend Dez and his little brother Uriah to light her life.

When Katrina is ordered to quash a rebel attack on the King's Command Center, she thinks it's just another job. But as she uncovers the plot, she is shocked to learn that Dez may be involved with the dissidents. Now Katrina must make an impossible choose—eliminate the one she loves, or defy the King she swore to serve.

The Spark is a sci-fi thriller about love, betrayal, and how the futures of others, even a whole civilization, can be determined through a single choice.

https://www.hiraethsffh.com/product-page/the-spark-by-stephen-c-curro

Gunpowder and Salt

Sharmon Gazaway

Again: turn, toe, turn, toe. Balan arched her arm overhead in fourth position, her feet in fifth. She smoothed the cameo pink tulle that fell from her waist in limp pleats, studied her form in the mirror, and frowned. "All gunpowder and salt," her Dear Parent often said. To her, about her to others.

She mimicked the pose in the 4-D holo-print of a Degas painting, the original destroyed long ago. Her parent had acquired it on the black-market after ballet had been outlawed for humans. He complained bitterly, and often, about the destruction of the arts, and the overreach of the Stellar Health Review.

Balan sprang, twirled on satin-shod toes—once, twice, fifty times in the silent studio, never tiring. Music flowed visually in a circuitous band around the hushed room, the wavelengths of light-music vibrating within her. She swanned, bowed, her fingers brushing the metalloid floor, her breast pressed flat against her thighs, folded like a pleated Degas fan.

The Dom, who Balan called Sylvie, rolled into the studio and watched her finish her *oeuvre*. Sylvie applauded by flashing all her lights green. She didn't use words, but they didn't need them. Sylvie's pulsing yellow light told Balan it was time for the recital, then she rolled out to serve the guests.

In front of the mirror, Balan tied a pink ribbon around the braid that snaked down her spine, smoothed her bangs flat against her forehead. She was the image of a fourteen-year-old dancer, the embodiment of a Degas sculpture.

Her Dear Parent appeared at the door. A tight smile cinched his lips. "Ah, my Balanchine. The guests are here!" He stroked his pointed gray beard. "Come, my dear." He held out his elbow to her, led her to the social arts hall and onto the genuine oak stage he'd paid dearly for.

A mere handful of the Intelligentsia that orbited her parent—and scientists like him—had been invited. They gathered around the stage, admiring the oak's warm sheen and envying her parent.

Mrs. Atlas smiled at Balan, her Astral Blonde 851 corkscrew curls bobbing beneath her fascinator. "My, Professor, she is a specimen. Your hard work is certainly evident."

"I'm unabashedly proud of her," he said over the splash of the lavish water feature, and gestured for them to sit.

Mr. Atlas sat beside Mrs. Atlas, who fussed with her bristly honey-gold skirt. Sylvie passed a tray of finger foods— zesty alpaca squares and vegellic sugar prisms—then rolled to the Dom station in front of a blank wall.

"Well done," Mr. Atlas said, nibbling the crunchy confection, brushing crumbs from his suit of black and white horizontal stripes. "Good domestics are impossible to find these days."

"Yes," agreed Mrs. Atlas. "I swear they've developed minds of their own."

"Well, there's a trick to that," the Professor said, winking.

There was no music. Music was considered gauche when one also had the extravagance of a water feature on this arid exoplanet. Entirely colonized by Elites, M1-576 had its perks, but an abundance of water was not one of them.

Her parent waved the light dim. Balan drew herself up. Her critical debut. Tonight she would make her Dear Parent proud. She took her position stage center.

To the right of the stage a holo of a famous dancer from the past, Misty Copeland, blinked to life. Balan hesitated. This was not what she had practiced.

Her parent signaled her to begin. Sans music, Balan's satin shoes whispered across the stage, en pointe. Pirouette, split leap, *fouette*! The guests' eyes followed her, bounced from her to the holo twirling beside the stage. Increasingly they focused on the holo of Copeland, and not on her.

Balan leapt tirelessly, drained every last ounce of her skill. She drew on all those nights when, after her parent had told her to retire, she'd secretly pirouetted and leapt and toed —how she had danced!

She flutter-toed across the wood, arched her back and arms in impossible angles. Chin to the air, neck taut, straining, straining.

"You do see, now, do you not?" Balan heard her Dear Parent say to Mrs. Atlas.

Mrs. Atlas nodded, her corkscrews trembling. "Did you not teach it to smile, Professor?"

He stroked his beard. "Oh, yes. It just wouldn't stick. I finally gave up and accepted her *'piquant de laideur'.*"

Instantly Balan stopped and bowed, forced her lips in an upward curve.

"Ah, yes, 'a spice of ugliness'." Mr. Atlas sighed.

"You were right, sir," Mrs. Atlas said. "About not being able to capture the elusive component of grace in its movements. Still, a prototype you can be proud of. AI has made great strides in your capable hands—the pursuit of true art, without the unnerving mechanics of the Doms."

"Even if she is all gunpowder and salt," Mr. Atlas said, and they laughed.

"My dear Balan, come forward."

Balan stepped up, hands clasped behind her.

"You are going with Mr. and Mrs. Atlas. They are moving to the unsettled colony, Machvel, and will need your help."

"Mars is a positive wilderness," said Mrs. Atlas.

This had not been part of Balan's recital practice. She ransacked her memory matrix. There was no algorithm for this situation. "For what measure of time?"

"Why, from now on, my dear. They have purchased you. They outbid all the others. They are fond of your spice of ugliness, I think. You are their new Dom. I'm sure you'll do well. No grace required." His eyes rested on her pink ribbon with what she recognized as sadness. And disappointment.

"W-will I—" She'd never stuttered before. A glitch. "Will you ever see me again?"

"Oh, no. I'm too old to be star-hopping. And besides, I will be much too busy engineering my new model." He smiled broadly. "Far superior."

"Do tell professor!"

"Well...she'll ply oils and brushes instead of toe-shoes."

"An AI artiste! Truly, you are a Renaissance Man!"

"Dear Parent, will I still be a dancer?" Balan blurted.

His eyes narrowed. "No. There's no need for that. Now is there?"

***

She was not allowed to take her things. Not her Degas holo-print, no tutus, not her pointe shoes with their much-fondled satin ribbons. She was given a Mars-issue black uniform.

As Balan followed the Atlases out, they passed by the Dom. Sylvie turned, faceless, to Balan, all her red lights flashing. She stared with filamentary eyes, then dropped her head.

The Future Adventures of
Bailey Belvedere

As the societies of Earth collapse into chaos and destruction, Bailey Belvedere, a U.S. Army Intelligence officer fighting for her very survival, steals aboard an alien spacecraft, and soon finds herself given the authority and power by a superior alien entity to intervene in various problems in the Galaxy. Along the way she frees a world from interstellar slave traffickers, deals with an AI who becomes pregnant, inadvertently destroys a waffle house, fights against the abductors of a special child, and generally finds herself in some sort of trouble from one moment to the next.

Type: Novel – science fiction

Ordering Links:
Print Edition: https://www.hiraethsffh.com/product-page/further-adventures-of-bailey-belvedere-by-tyree-campbell

PDF Edition: https://www.hiraethsffh.com/product-page/further-adventures-of-bailey-belvedere-by-tyree-campbell-1

Movie review: In My Mother's Skin

Lee Clark Zumpe

'In My Mother's Skin' is a beguiling, bleak & grim foray into folk horror

Desperate situations demand desperate remedies — or so we have been told, since at least the age of Hippocrates, the famous Greek physician. Under particularly adverse circumstances, one might embrace actions they would normally reject as excessive or immoral. When confronted with an urgent predicament, it may become necessary to pursue an extreme or unconventional course of action — one which may conflict with a person's nature or personal values.

In folklore, desperation often compels a victim to turn to supernatural agents for aid and comfort. Unfortunately, this often leads to an impossible choice.

There are many examples of the impossible choice in mythology and folktales. There is the miller in "The Girl Without Hands" who — having made a Mephistophelian bargain — must choose between being carted off by the devil or chopping off his daughter's hands; or more famously, there's the girl in "Rumpelstiltskin" who's given a choice between certain death and handing over her firstborn child to a creepy, gold-spinning imp.

Whether it's a fairy tale pulled from the Grimm brothers' "Children's and Household Tales" or folk narratives and fables from non-Western cultures, these stories reflect the real world, in which individuals may unexpectedly come face-to-face with an overwhelming ordeal and may be forced to make an impossible choice.

Daily headlines are a constant reminder that despite all the remarkable progress we have made as a species, we still cling to our savage predilection for committing acts of brutality and mass atrocity. We still thoughtlessly inflict trauma and suffering, pushing people into desperation.

This theme is depicted eloquently in the macabre new folk horror film "In My Mother's Skin," written and directed by Kenneth Dagatan. Having made its premiere at Sundance in January, this transfixing cinematic fable was acquired by Amazon Studios and debuted Oct. 12 on Prime Video.

"In My Mother's Skin" is both beautiful and excruciatingly bleak. It clearly evokes the tone and imagination of Guillermo del Toro's far superior "Pan's Labyrinth," but it does not come across as a derivative pastiche. Dagatan juxtaposes the manifest horrors of war with the maliciousness of a malevolent entity.

The story takes place on a remote estate in the Philippines during the final days of World War II. The mansion is the home of what was once a wealthy and influential family who are now struggling to survive during the period of Japanese occupation. The hopelessness and urgency of their situation is made clear from the start when Tala (Felicity Kyle Napuli), the family's adolescent daughter, tells her little brother Bayani (James Mavie Estrella) that she had heard stories about Japanese soldiers tossing Philippine babies into the air and impaling them on their bayonets.

Hoping to enlist the help of American soldiers, the children's father Romualdo (Arnold Reyes) leaves the home, even though his wife Ligaya (Beauty Gonzalez) is clearly too sickly to care for the children. As Ligaya's condition quickly deteriorates, Tala realizes the family will soon run out of food to eat. She feels she must act to ensure the survival of the family.

Despite her mother's protests, Tala and Bayani set out into the forest surrounding the estate, hoping to reach a nearby village. On their journey, each child is confronted with something horrific: Bayani finds a gully filled with the corpses of villagers summarily executed by the Japanese. Tala discovers a secluded hut in the woods — a creepy little cottage with stained glass windows that may not be made of gingerbread and candy, but it still evokes the dwelling of a certain cannibalistic witch who tempted Hansel and Gretel with treats.

Inside the hut, Tala encounters a mysterious fairy (Jasmine Curtis-Smith) who offers to protect her and to grant her wishes. The fairy provides her with a magical bug she claims will cure her mother. She implies there may be a cost for this gift of life, but Tala is so desperate to save her mother she takes no notice.

The bug does its job: Ligaya's illness disappears. In its place, she develops a long, proboscis-like tongue and an insatiable urge to consume flesh. Graphic carnage follows as the parasitic bug controlling Tala's mother becomes increasingly ravenous and all traces of Ligaya's humanity gradually become eclipsed by cannibalistic hunger.

The fairy reminds Tala that she made a choice. There's always a catch.

Dagatan's deceitful fairy is part trickster and part vampire. The entity seems to be modeled after the vampiric aspect of the Tagalog "aswang," a bloodsucking creature disguised as a beautiful maiden. Maximo Ramos, in "The Aswang Syncrasy in Philippine Folklore, writes that according to folk traditions, "to suck blood the vampire uses the tip of its tongue, pointed like the proboscis of a mosquito, to pierce the jugular vein." In J. Gordon Melton's "The Vampire Book," the author notes that the term "aswang" applied to a set of different creatures, including werewolves, ghouls, and vampires. In its vampiric state, it could transform into a bird, fly through the night to the home of its intended victim, and perch on the roof while using its long tongue to feast. Children were warned to stay inside at night to avoid being attacked by one of these creatures.

The director cleverly uses elements of this folktale in the film. The invasive nature of the parasitic insect can be considered a metaphor for how the Philippine population suffered during the Japanese occupation. In a broader sense, the story is a blanket condemnation of colonization and imperialism.

Dagatan delivers this compelling, tragically timely social commentary without diminishing the film's ability to terrify and disturb viewers. The cast's work is admirable overall, but it is Napuli's portrayal of Tala that makes all this work. As Tala, she wears a mask of noble grace to hide her resigned despondency. Her innocence makes her reliable as a witness to existential threats, whether it's the prospect of slow death by starvation or falling victim to a supernatural entity. Although the viewer may find some consolation in seeing how much Tala is capable of enduring, the final lines she speaks serve as a haunting requiem for innocence lost.

"In My Mother's Skin" is a blood-drenched dark fantasy set against a nightmarish dreamscape of war and despair. It successfully blends history, folklore, and graphic horror to create a beguiling, shocking tale of war and tragedy.

Lee Clark Zumpe is entertainment editor at Tampa Bay Newspapers, a Tomatometer-Approved Critic, and an author of short fiction appearing in select anthologies and magazines. Follow Lee at www.patreon.com/Haunter_of_the_Bijou.

Whispers from the
Intoxicating Abyss
By Lee Clark Zumpe

You may not realize it, but they're out there: impossible shadows, omniscient horrors, and unseen, unknowable entities scattered across the great gulfs of nothingness at the edges of the universe. In this collection, author Lee Clark Zumpe draws back the curtain from the invisible realm, divulging its arcane secrets and ghastly revelations. Come walk paths meandering over shunned worlds adrift in darkness, and through seemingly mundane, liminal spaces that might be overrun with ancient shadows at any moment.

Stories are inspired by the works of H. P. Lovecraft.

Ordering links:
Print: https://www.hiraethsffh.com/product-page/whispers-from-the-intoxicating-abyss-by-lee-clark-zumpe

ePub: https://www.hiraethsffh.com/product-page/whispers-from-the-intoxicating-abyss-by-lee-clark-zumpe-2

PDF: https://www.hiraethsffh.com/product-page/whispers-from-the-intoxicating-abyss-by-lee-clark-zumpe-1

The Wolves of Glastonbury
by Edward Cox & Terrie Leigh Relf

What happens in Glastonbury stays in Glastonbury—even if it means the end of one of humanity's longest alternate lifelines. The hunt is on for Claire and Ethan . . .

https://www.hiraethsffh.com/product-page/wolves-of-glastonbury-by-terrie-leigh-relf-edward-cox

Feast Day
Hersh Solomon Jr.

Before sunrise, Mayfair the Pig woke up from a strange and enormous dream. His large, porcine eyes opened to see a great, blue comet searing across the sky. The sight of it filled him with melancholy, bringing a tear to his eye. Something about the dream he had and the sight of the comet he saw, spelled inside him a question, whose answer the likes of which was only beginning to fathom. A sense of mourning from all the cruelty that his kind had suffered over the years incited his sense of agony. Looking at the sky again, the comet filled his eyes. His pupils glistened. One big tear, for all the pigs who'd died.

Something inside him felt different. He felt *alive.* A new consciousness dawned inside his mind. When he was born, he couldn't tell the difference between a pig and a human. It was only later that he perceived it. But now, that difference had overlapped. After having been mistreated over the years and aggravated by Farmer Johns' neglect to the well-being of the animals on the farm, it was surely Mayfair who was the humane one, not him. He may be a pig, but he was charming, frank, and quick-witted, certainly not a *murderer* like Farmer John.

In him kindled a sense of the desire for justice. Mayfair rolled his tongue in contemplation of the word. From the henhouse rose the rambling of the rooster, his ordinary morning speech bubbling up into a high spot. Something about the tone of his voice told Mayfair that the rooster was thinking the same thing as him.

He lolled about in the mud. The thick, cooling sensation was relaxing. His massive hide ploughed the soft earth of the pen. It wasn't easy being a pig.

Over the gently rolling hills of Plankton Farm, the light of dawn arose. In the farmhouse, Farmer John was fast asleep. His snoring was interspersed with bursts of incoherent mumbling. He was dreaming. Usually, he slept like a log, but this night had been full of fits and spurts.

A zealous squawking from the henhouse roused him. Genevieve slept soundly beside him. On the wall hung a picture of his great grandfather, Bluey, standing in front of the henhouse. The very same henhouse that the chooks were squawking in now. They could feel it, and so could he: It was *Feast Day*. A sense of nervous excitement filled the air. Something was going to happen. Something always happened on Feast Day.

He got out of bed and opened the shutters, letting the morning light in. Rows of tables and chairs had been set up in the yard between the house and the barn. The jumping castle was pegged down and ready to be inflated. Speakers and a microphone had been set up for the speeches. There were spaces dotted all around the farm containing and displaying pieces of memorabilia denoting the history of the area. As John put on his hat, the rooster named Pinchos let rip with an almighty crow from the henhouse, and this was followed with a raucous squawking which gave John cause to curse.

"Vieve,' he said, putting on some sunscreen.

'Yes, dear?' she murmured from bed.

'It's Feast Day.'

'I know,' she said.

He put on his boots and looked in the mirror. He could see the likeness of Bluey looking proudly back at him.

John tied up his bootstraps and headed down the stairs. 'Danny!'

'What?!' came Danny's voice from out the back.

'Don't forget to inflate the jumping castle!'

'Okay!' Danny said.

On the veranda, John looked up at the early morning sky. There, streaking across the atmosphere, was a giant white comet, leaving a long blue-tail behind it, like a river in the sky.

He stepped off the veranda to go to the henhouse to check on the chicken. A car coming down the road cut him off before he got there. The car pulled up in a cloud of dust and a man wearing square glasses stepped out. It was Wayne. 'Are the delicacies ready to go?' he asked after shaking John's hand.

'Yes,' he said sternly. 'Just don't talk about it. Don't even think about it.'

Wayne was a scientist who'd been snubbed for his lack of ethics regarding the use of stem cell technology. The two of them had been working together for the past six months. Using biological embryos to hasten the development of tastiness in the livestock, they had gone on to genetically engineer a new species of bird that contained all the best tasting meats all combined into one flesh. These birds were riper, plumper, juicier, fatter, and tastier than any other variety of livestock. Just the thought of the taste of them was enough to get John salivating right now.

With the mercury rising, John took off his hat and wiped his brow. It was a nerve-wracking business, this sneaking around so that they were not caught. But he was motivated to stay ahead of the market. 'Relax,' said Wayne. 'We've got our government man, now. It's three months until the next election. If we just lay low for the next couple of months, by the time they discover them, the new laws will be in, which allow cell technologies for meat production.'

'Are you sure?'

'Absolutely. It's more humane to use stem cells to make meat than to slaughter living animals.'

John nodded.

In a locked basement beneath the shed, he kept them. These biologically engineered tastiest delights. Huddled in cages, their feathers' flurry of colours revealed their flavours. For the past six months, they had been getting tastier and tastier with each generation. The deliciousness of the meat validated the purpose of their creation. Using cover funds to pay for the equipment, they had set up the lab beneath the barn. The first generation had been a failure, the birds had self-cannibalized, pecking themselves to death. A few changes in the genes regulating aggressiveness had fixed the problem. The moment they cooked the meat and put it on a plate, they could tell from the smell of it that they were on to something good. It was a chicken with a pig mixed in with its genes. Slowly but surely, they eased in beef; then duck; goat, and sheep. The final product was a six-foot beast that was unlike any animal they had seen before.

And the taste! Each bite of the tender meat these hybrids produced was a triumph of the palette. John was sure it would revolutionize the meat industry. All the other meats on the market would become obsolete.

He went around the cages and gave them their morning fare and care. In a small segmented off area at the back, there was a covered fry pan on a small stove. They went in and John produced a couple of skewers of the tender meat he'd fried earlier, and they shared it. Wayne gasped the moment he tasted it, unable to express the delight the meat gave him. The moment anyone got a taste of these hybrids, all discontent about the ethics of the stem-cells used to breed them was sure to vanish.

Taking some tranquilizer medicine out of the cabinet, he distributed it among the hybrids, to keep them settled. They were the size of ostriches; more voluptuous. The last thing they would need would be for them to get themselves in a calling frenzy. They had beaks the size of ducks that were capable of very loud quacking.

They left the basement and locked the doors. The stallion, Stomper, was feeding on hay in the shed. Wayne gave him a pat on the back, and they walked outside, where the shimmering heat glistened gently against the grassy horizon. On the hill, Danny was inflating the jumping castle. Genevieve had drunk a cup of tea on the porch and was now headed to the tables to get them ready.

John and Wayne crossed the yard to the henhouse when a sudden honk from the gates caught their eye. A small parade of cars was coming down the hill. John stopped short and caught his breath. He grabbed Wayne by the arm. 'We have got to get the meat ready!' They went back inside the house to the refrigerators, where several plates of some of the choicest cuts of their newfound delicacies were stashed away. John heated up the meat in the microwave and put it all in a couple of large pots. 'Here,' he said, giving one to Wayne. He looked at him. 'For *adults* only,' he said.

Wayne took the pot. 'Are you kidding? It's for *every*body. There's no reason why a child should have to miss out on this inspiringly tasty, healthy new brand of genetically engineered meat, just because they are young, is there?'

'Just phase it in,' said John.

Outside, the guests had arrived. John took the pot, with some char-grilled steaks of the magic meat provided by the hybrids and offered it to a reporter from the local newspaper. 'What is this?' he asked.

'Special treat,' said John. He offered the pot to them. The reporter took a fork from the side of the dish and put it into a steak. He sniffed. It looked like chicken. Smelt like chicken, only superior. He put the portion into his mouth and took a bite. *'Hmm,'* he said, chewing. Then, taking another bite, 'That's delicious. What is it?'

'Secret ingredient,' John pointed with a wink.

From the barn, there was another bout of loud squawking. 'Excuse me,' said John, handing the bowl to the reporter. 'Pass it round.'

'Feast daaayy!' cawed Pinchos the Rooster with his claw pointed high. All about the henhouse, the chooks were in a rattle. Pinchos the Rooster, talkative at the worst of times, had awoken this morning to find in his cockles a speech the likes of which he'd never spoken before. An elder statesman among the many animals on the farm, they had all grown used to the sound off the loins of his throat that sounded throughout the paddocks at sunrise every morning. Come rain, hail, or shine, you could always count on Pinchos to get the chatter going.

He bobbed his head, strutting back and forth in indignation. *'Beast* day, more like it! A celebration of murderers of the age-long persecution of all animalia, right across the board! There isn't an animal on earth that hasn't felt the sharp bite of steel from a human's hand. But they are no better than us! Nay, not one bit. They *need* us! But as for us, we don't need *them!* Why should we tolerate for even one more instant this insanity? To do so would be to enter an eternal regression to our own detriment. It's madness, I'm telling you. Madness!'

Around the pen, several chickens were scratching their heads in thoughtful provocation. All around, the conscious levels of the animals had gone up. There was a light that had been switched on in their souls, and they could all see it.

Pinchos had had enough of it. 'I don't know about you, but I'm not about to just stand by and passively observe as these unconscionable humans celebrate their prolonged torture of our misery. Not just ours, but all animalia's! It's time to take a stand.'

'He's not so bad!' said one of the hens. 'Farmer John's all right. It's *me* that you have got to worry about!' A group of hens clucked acquiescently. 'I'm the *really* nasty one!' They clucked again.

No,' said one of the other hens seriously. 'We are *more* than just meat. You, with your sense of humour; there's no other hen who has the type of humour the likes of which you do. And *you,*' she went to another chicken. '*All* of us. We're all different. We should all start to express our own personalities, from now on. Like humans do. We're just as much the characters as them.'

'We have *all* been relegated to a level below savage by the sheer arrogance of our cruel human masters,' decried Pinchos from his perch. 'It's gone on so long, we have come to think we deserve it. But it is not right, I tell you. On a grand, cosmic scale, it is just not right!'

They had worked up such a stir in the henhouse that other animals were beginning to appear from their pens. Pinchos motioned to the sheep. 'You! I have seen you suffering mightily recently with a bad case of fleas, but does Farmer John do anything about it? *Noooooooo!*' There was another uproar. 'And you, Stomper,' he said to the Stallion, whose presence cast a shadow at the entrance of the henhouse door. 'You know how the story goes. First, they grind you into the dust from backbreaking work from dusk to dawn from day one. Then, when you're no longer useful, you're off to the knackers without a pretence of any kind of sentiment!' Pinchos' speech had the animals worked up. They were on the verge of revolting.

Just then, the big doors at the front of the henhouse burst open and Farmer John barged in, shouting, and clapping clamorously. 'Righto! Righto! Righto! It's *Feast Day!*' His entranced sent the chickens into a sprawl.

"*How daaaaaare* you!" crowed Pinchos, shaking his claw familiarly.

'Out! Out! Out! Out! Out!' said John, stomping his feet. He went around smacking the larger animals on the rump, clearing them out.

"*This* is what I'm *talking about*,' cawed Pinchos hoarsely. 'The unconscionable lack of respect afforded to his most prized possessions upon which his living relies!' But he was losing them. The exits had been cleared and the chooks were entering into freefall through the door and down the ramp into the pen. 'If only this man would attempt to listen, that we could teach him some things. But he won't! He never will!'

John tried to grab him, but Pinchos evaded his grasp. 'Stop it, Rooster!' he yelled, going after him.

Jose, one of the younger roosters, crowed and spread his wings triumphantly. Emboldened by a sense of duty, he jumped onto John's back and clawed his shoulders. John rocked back and grabbed Jose by the neck, sending a shrill shriek through the rooster's throat. '*What* on *earth* has gotten into you?' he shouted. Carrying Jose across the pen, he said, 'Oh, yeah. I remember. It's *Feast Day!*' He tossed the Rooster unceremoniously out.

Mayfair, standing staunchly at the back entrance door to the henhouse, unemotionally observed everything that was going on. The pain, the anger, the strife. Their eternal torment. Outside, he was there, on the same farm that his mother and father had trod upon. But inside, he was a long, long way away.

When he was just a wee piglet, Genevieve had picked him up and met his eyes, and he had instantly fallen in love. It was the single greatest and most inexpressible moment of his short, inglorious life. He'd thought that the sole purpose of their dual existence was to come into this world to meet each other and be together. Later, he'd learned the harsh indignity at the truth of his naive ambitions. She was a woman. A *human,* with a spirit, and a conscience, and a personality, and all that. And he was nothing but a pig. A fat, dirty pig, the butt of all their cruel jokes. There was no way they could ever be together.

He was jolted rudely back to the present moment by the sharp stun of the electric prodder that John used to annoy him with whenever he got off onto a long train of thought. 'Morning, sunshine!' said John, holding the prodder out to his side, clicking with electric current. 'Off you go,' he said, approaching him again with prodder pointed. Mayfair thought about it. After a few moments of consideration, he plodded out.

'You're obsolete, now,' said John on his way off.

Mayfair stopped in his tracks; his ears perked up. Did he hear him right? Did he say *obsolete?*

Outside, the festivities were in full swing. The tables had filled up with guests. The gypsy band had arrived, and the sound of the violin swung in the meadows. Gregarious bouts of laughter from the guests fuelled the music's cause. It was all happening. And as for the serves of the hybrid meat dishes, they couldn't get enough of it. After finishing the first pots, they had demanded more. Wayne had inconspicuously gone to the back of the freezer to retrieve the rest of the supply that they had on hand, and given it to Genevieve, who was now frying it on a stove top outside. A group of onlookers looked on expectantly, rubbing their hands and licking their lips.

John briskly went to the front of the tables, greeting people cheerfully along the way. 'What's happened here?' asked one of them, touching the tear in the shoulder of his shirt.

'What, this?' asked John, touching his shoulder to reveal blood. He looked at his hand. 'I will tell you what it is,' he said. 'It's *Feast Day!* You can expect the unexpected.'

Another guest came up to him. 'John!' they said. 'Where did you get the new meat?'

He touched his nose. 'Trade secret.'

'We run a restaurant in a nearby town. We'd love to have it!'

'Good,' said John. 'We'll see what we can do. Thank you.'

The jumping castle was fully inflated, and it bounced lightly in the breeze that was picking up from the hills. At the stove, the meat was fried, and Genevieve was serving it up. The delight in the eyes of the reactions of those who ate it spoke more than words ever could.

A shiny Mercedes came through the gate and made its way down the dirt road. Wayne appeared at John's side, who was sharpening his wits in preparation to make a speech. 'Government agent's here,' he said.

John nodded. 'Danny!' he called.

Danny came over from supervising the jumping castle.

'Go and welcome the government man. Make him feel comfortable.'

Wayne put his hand on John's shoulder. 'Bluey would be proud of you, mate.' With his other hand, he took a bite of the scrumptious hybrid meat he was eating. *'Mmm,'* he moaned.

The government agent was greeted by Danny, and they came over. '...Our chickens are the best on the market,' Danny was saying.

'John McRonald,' said the government agent, holding out his hand. 'Thomas Donaldson.'

John smiled widely and shook Thomas's hand. 'Glad you could make it.'

'Pleasure to be here,' said Thomas. Then, quietly, 'Do you have something to show me?'

'Yes,' said John, looking around conspicuously. 'Follow me.'

He led Thomas to the underground storehouse of hybrids. Wayne followed. He switched on the light, revealing them in their hundreds. 'So,' said Thomas, 'Here they are.'

'Yes. Now, when can we expect to get a contract?'

'Be patient,' Thomas said. 'We have been lobbying for the use to stem cell technology to come in behind the scenes. It's only a matter of time before the animal rights campaigners come to agree with us. Don't worry, you will get your contract.'

'We would like a bit more of a guarantee,' said Wayne. 'We're taking a big risk, here.'

'Don't worry,' said Thomas. 'The moment the new government forms in a few months' time, you will get reimbursed for the money you have spent so far. *Plus,* funds for further development. Then will come the contract, to exclusively provide the hybrid meat to the whole state. Then the nation. It's only a matter of time.'

Just then, a rattling from the stairs alerted them to an intruder. It was the reporter from the local newspaper. He bumped his head on the door as he came in. Then, looking around, said, 'What is *this?*'

John looked at him, gobsmacked. Wayne began stuttering. Thomas, taking control, spoke authoritatively. 'This is classified government business, none of your concern.'

'This is inhumane treatment of animals!' said the reporter, looking around. 'Why, I ought to report this to the animal welfare agency. What on earth *are* these things.'

Thomas took him by the arm and began leading him back up the stairs. 'These *things* are the tastiest animals known to humankind yet! They're going to revolutionise the market. Now, don't tell anyone about it, and we will give you the scoop, understand?'

As they left the barn, from an inconspicuous shadow, Mayfair was watching them. Something about John's comment was irking him. He could tell from the looks on the faces of the men that something was afoot under the barn. Picking a moment when no one was watching, Mayfair walked around the back side, where a latched door sealed the entrance. Standing upright on hind legs, he manipulated the latch with his trotter until he was able to get it loose.

The horse ignored him as he snuck in and went to the door that led down to the cellar. He tried to open it but was unable. 'Trotter,' he asked, 'Do you know anything about this?' Trotter snorted wind out of his nose, indicating that he refused to answer.

Just then, a rat came out from underneath the door and scrambled along the edge of the wall. 'Hey!,' said Mayfair, 'You there!' The rat turned from the corner and looked at him. 'Who? Me?'

Mayfair walked around the rat. 'Yes. I was wondering if you could tell me what lies down there in the cellar.'

The rat chewed on it for a moment. 'What's in it for me?' Mayfair thought about it. 'Tell you what,' said the rat, 'If you will let me have a little bit of Stomper's food over there, I will tell you.'

Mayfair went into a bargaining process with Stomper, and eventually convinced him to give the rat some of his food on the grounds that he would owe him a favour.

'Thanks,' said the rat, then he scurried back under the door again.

'Hey!' said Mayfair, trying to stop him, but his trotter was too uncoordinated to do so. A minute later, the rat reappeared. In his claw, he carried a feather, which he handed to Mayfair. Looking at it, he saw that it was unlike any other feather that he'd seen. 'Where did you get this?'

The rat proceeded to tell him about the hybrids. How the humans had been genetically engineering them for the past six months. How they had grown into their current form. Now Mayfair knew what John had meant when he had called him obsolete. Mayfair went and told Pinchos, who had spread the word around to the other animals. Upon hearing the news, they began preparing to take action.

On the makeshift podium, Farmer John stepped up to give a speech. 'Since my grandfather, Bluey, came and settled this farm, the town around it has grown to thrive. The tastier our animals are, the better everything gets. And now, thanks to a new government contract that is on the horizon, things are going to get even better. We are going to be selling our meat to the whole nation!' A round of applause was accompanied by cheering and whistling.

Just then, an insane chicken stampede the likes of which no one had seen before came barnstorming out of the henhouse, cutting John off in mid-sentence. Pinchos Rooster led from the front. 'The gate!' he crowed.

Mayfair, startled by the intensity of the ruckus, lost himself for a moment, then recovered and used his sturdy rump to bump the gate, but it would not open. He bumped it again; the chains rattled, almost coming unstuck. By now the stampeding mob of chickens were almost upon him. Pinchos Rooster, in a spectacular display of athleticism, rose up off the ground and flew through the air, clearing the gate with room to spare. The next bump broke the gates' chains in the nick of time, and the chickens came storming through.

The mob of berserk chickens swarmed into the crowd. They jumped onto people's laps as they sat at the tables and pecked at them indiscriminately. A wave of awe and amazement swept through the rest of the animalian ranks.

'Don't just stand there!' said John, 'Do something!' The humans snapped out of their stupefaction and into action. Mothers ran to their children. Fathers came to the front line to defend them from the onrushing chickens with kicks of their boots and swinging chairs. Danny got the shotgun and blasted a few rounds into the air. But there was no subduing the animals' frenzy. Emboldened by the success the chickens were having, a flock of sheep barged past Mayfair and into the fray, causing tables, chairs, and people to go flying.

An urge came over Mayfair to stand on his hind legs. It seemed like a natural thing to do. He hopped his front legs up to the lower upright of a nearby fence. Then up again. He carefully balanced on his hind legs and took a few steps backward and forward until he got his balance. He picked up a pitchfork which was leaning against the fence and held it aloft. 'Enough's enough!'

'*Mooooooo!*' The cows, whose udders had been milked raw, entered the fray. They bulldozed a sizeable portion of the crowd, then turned back around for another run.

One of the goats made contact with the gas stove that was set up beside the tables, causing it to tip over. The flame fell onto the tablecloths, setting them on fire. Now that they had their attention, suddenly the humans began to hear the animals speaking in plain English. 'Oh, *now* you understand, do you?' taunted Pinchos as he pecked away at a petrified guest.

Mayfair saw Thomas opening his bag and pulling out a mobile phone. He charged him and knocked him asunder. The phone flew out of his hands.

Pinchos Rooster hopped up to the dais in the midst of the carnage and raised his beak to the sky. '*Cockadoodledoo!*' The sound rang over the rolling paddocks of the farm. The fire had spread across the table cloths, and smoke was billowing into the sky.

Galvanized by the success they were having, the animalian ranks had their tails up. So incensed were they, that even the free animals, who had been mere bystanders thus far, went completely feral and joined the assault. Birds, bats, possums, spiders, snakes, all joined in the fray. Even the dog, who's loyalty had held him off, got carried away, and begun attacking its masters. The only one who remained unmoved was the cat, who watched on from the porch in befuddlement.

Mayfairs' ears flicked up from the orchard, he heard Genevieve screaming. He lurched over by the barn and found her clutching a meat cleaver as a brood of bloodthirsty cows swamped her. 'Get away from her!' he yelled.

'Mayfair!' said Genevieve, stunned. 'You can talk!'

'I can do a lot more than that,' he said. 'The time has come to show you the pig I really am.' He paraded around the cows, swinging the pitchfork, causing them to disperse.

Genevieve fainted; Mayfair scooped her up in his trusty trotters before she hit the ground. Her eyes gleamed as she looked up at him upon his arrival. Such was Mayfair's joy at this fantastic turn of events that he was overwhelmed, and he swung Genevieve around and threw her up in the air with delight. 'Mayfair!' she screamed.

'We won!' he yelled simultaneously as he caught her in his arms. She pulled away the thicket of hair that had fallen in front of her face and they looked at each other. Daring to believe, Mayfair seized the moment and leaned in, kissing her gently. An awkward smile spread across her face. 'Genevieve, my dear. There's been a revolution. Come with me.'

Sensing the bloodthirstiness of the animalian revolt, she said, 'No!'

'Don't worry. I'll protect you.' He held out his arm. 'Come, dear.'

Back in the yard, disorder reigned unchecked. Mayfair raised his pitchfork. His shadow stretched across the scene: 'Freedom!' he bellowed.

The *sprong* of a pellet from the shotgun bouncing off his pitchfork caused him to momentarily lose his balance. Another pellet *zoomed* by his ear.

'*You're dead meat,*' came the voice of Danny.

Stomper galloped completely unannounced from the thicket and with a tremendous *neighing* thrust forward. He headbutted Danny, who sprawled asunder, sending *the* shotgun flying. Mayfair wiped the sweat from his brow. 'Thanks, Stomper,' he said. 'That's two I owe you now.'

The shed wall burst open and a van with Wayne behind the wheel came thundering out. The van accelerated with a fiery roar and came up the hill. It swivelled out of control, toppled over, and flipped spectacularly.

The swarming animals now outnumbered the humans. John and a small group of others fled across the grounds to the house, defending their entrance with their spades and picks, and locked himself in. The animals surrounded them.

'*Leave us alone!*' came the voice of John from through the second story window of the house.

'*You're going to pay for all the animals that have suffered on this farm!*' retorted Pinchos, causing an uproar.

Mayfair heard the steadfast gallop of Stomper's hooves from behind. He barely had time to dive out of the way before the stallion, mane flaying in the wind, barged past. He rammed into the door of the house, smashing it, and the animalian ranks swarmed it.

Minutes later, Farmer John was taken out. A cross was erected on the spot, and the possums used their dextrous hands to nail him to it. The other hostages were tied up and made to stand next to him. The animals gathered around John as he hung from the cross.

Word of the events on Plankton Farm spread into the surrounding regions, causing an influx of animals and humans from all around. The animals had won, and now they looked to consolidate their victory. 'We need a judge!' said Mayfair.

'I'm scared, May-may,' said Genevieve.

'Don't be afraid,' said Mayfair, 'I'm with you.'

A flustered, sweaty man with thin, balding red hair, clearly dishevelled, was jostled into the room. 'Are you the magistrate?' Mayfair asked him.

'I'm a magistrate, but I'm not qualified to adjudicate on this, p-preposterousness.'

'Yes, you are,' said Mayfair. He swept off a heap of dishes from a table, and shuffled the magistrate into a chair behind a makeshift bench. The animals were worked up, making a loud noise. Mayfair used the pitchfork to get their attention. 'Quiet down!' he yelled. Once the noise had settled, he turned to the magistrate. 'Look, mate,' said Mayfair, 'This is *our* farm.'

'Animals don't have the right to own land.'

They decided to create a Declaration of Animals Rights in order to legally qualify them for ownership of the farm. Mayfair held the draft aloft and read: 'We hold these truths to be self-evident, that all animals are created equal, and have a right to life, liberty and the pursuit of happiness. All animals have the same natural right to exist, to be free, and to live on their own terms. All animals have the right to eat, sleep, be physically and psychologically comfortable, be mobile, healthy, safe, and fulfil all their natural and essential needs. As such, all animals are to be free from hunger, thirst, and malnutrition; physical discomfort and exhaustion; confinement against their will, bad treatment, abusive or cruel actions; pain, injury, and disease; fear and distress; and free to express their normal patterns of behaviour. All animals have the right to reproduce, live with their offspring, families, tribes, or communities, and maintain a natural social life. They have the right to live in their natural environment, grow to a rhythm natural to their species, and maintain a life that corresponds to their natural longevity. Animals are not the property or commodity of humans and are not theirs to use for their benefit or sustenance. Therefore, they are to be free from slavery, exploitation, oppression, victimization, brutality, abuse, and any other treatment that disregards their safety, own free will and dignity. Humans shall do whatever is within their means to protect all animals. Any animal who is dependent on a human, has the right to proper sustenance and care, and shall not be neglected, abandoned, or killed. Animals who have died must be treated with respect and dignity, as humans are. We call for the protection of these rights. They must be recognized and defended by law, as human rights are. Any act which compromises the wellbeing or survival of an animal or species, or jeopardizes, contradicts, or deprives an animal or species of the rights listed above, should be deemed a crime, and should be punished accordingly.'

Magistrate Baldock, stunned at the gravity of the declaration, sat gobsmacked behind the bench, unable to act out on his magisterial duties. Mayfair looked menacingly at him. Magistrate Baldock hastily nodded his head and knocked his mallet. 'Animalia and Humankind are now equal under the law. These animals now not only have their freedom, but they also have ownership of Plankton Farm.' An almighty cheer went up.

Wayne wiped his eyes. He put his hand on Mayfair's shoulder. 'I'm sorry. For all the suffering we have caused to you and your kind.'

Mayfair clicked his heels. 'Apology accepted, my good chap.'

Just then, it became strangely dark. The sun's light was being muffled by the comet, which had grown ominously large in the sky. The air reverberated and swirled; lightning crackled, and thunder rumbled. A schism oscillated in the stratosphere, and a whirlpool opened in the sky. Looking closely at the whirlpool, it appeared to be a portal to another world.

The wind blew a gale, became a hurricane, and water from the comet began pouring in. Genevieve wrapped her arms around Mayfair and clung to him for dear life. 'What's happening, May-May?'

A crooked smile spread itself across his lips. 'Why, it's a celebration, my love,' he said. 'The heavens are throwing a party, and we're the guests of honour.' An explosion of air and water broke open a hole in the sky, and a whirlpool descended onto the ground, shattering everything outside of it asunder. He squinted his large eyes and looked up. Thousands upon thousands of birds of all kinds flew around in the sky in an ocean of wings. They were departing from the Earth, flying through the planetary portal, which swam as a whirlpool in the sky.

'*Fly them out!*' screamed Wayne, as he was being carried away, off the ground, by the voluminous winds. '*The hybrids!*' He flew up into the air, and was tossed hither and tither.

Mayfair ran to the barn and went down into the cellar. Moving swiftly through the aisles of cages, he unlatched them as he went, and out came the six-foot rainbow coloured hybrid chickens. One by one, they went up the stairs. Upon exiting the barn, they took to flight like a fleet of warplanes. They flew around the farm for a minute and then came to ground, kneeling in order to allow themselves to be mounted.

All the humans in the area began mounting the rainbow hybrids, who flew them up and away, through the portal that had opened up to Neptune. Mayfair gallantly ran to one of them who lay on the ground. 'Ladies, first,' he said, putting Genevieve on its back. But before he could mount it himself, one of the guests came along and pushed him over, sending him sprawling. 'Humans before animals,' he said, jumping behind Genevieve. The hybrid unfurled its wings and took to the air.

'*Mayfair!*' screamed Genevieve.

Mayfair righted himself and looked up. The hybrid was already twelve feet in the air.

'Jump, my darling!' he yelled. 'Jump!'

Genevieve jumped from the hybrid and fell into his strong arms. They kissed and she hugged him tightly. 'May?'

'Yes, darling?'

'I just thought of something?'

'What is it, my love?'

'Well...I was thinking that maybe this is all just a dream.'

'Maybe it is. But if that's true, I don't ever want to wake up.'

'Neither do I.' She closed her eyes and hugged him tightly.

On the ground, a tremendous earthquake began to rattle the earth. Down the centre of the farm, an enormous crack began to appear.

He ran over to another hybrid lying in wait. But just as they were about to mount, a woman in high heels trod on his foot. 'Ouch!'

'Who do you think you are?' she asked as she mounted the hybrid and flew away.

'Never mind, my dear,' he said. 'There's plenty more where that came from.'

He bounded in the direction of another hybrid.

'All my life, I thought us humans were so smart,' said Genevieve. 'But it turns out that we were the animals all along, and the animals are the civilized ones.'

They arrived at the hybrid. 'Safety, at last,' said Mayfair. His vision shattered in an explosion of agony as Farmer John whacked him over the head with his cross. 'It should've been you,' said John, as he mounted the hybrid and flew away.

A lump rose on his head. Despite the pain, and the accompanying dizziness, Mayfair righted himself, collected his bearings, and carried Genevieve in another direction. There were only a few hybrids left. Mayfair galloped in a last-ditch effort to the nearest one, but right at the last moment, he was tripped over by Stomper. 'You owe me,' said Stomper, who mounted the hybrid and took off. Mayfair looked up into the sky as the hybrid carrying Stomper flew away, and through the planetary portal.

All the hybrids were gone. The portal to the other world closed off.

That evening, alone amidst what was left of the farm, Mayfair the Pig and Genevieve stood in the high corn, watching the sun set on Feast Day.

'Mayfair?'

'Yes, dear?'

'Are we in heaven?'

'It's not quite heaven, my love,' he said, 'But it is very, very pleasant.'

The Earth was theirs. They'd be lonely, but it was a small price to pay. He looked up, wise old pig that he was, into the sky, looking for any hybrids still around. He didn't think there would be, but he never knew. *Maybe they'll come back for us,* he thought.

You had to have hope. Mayfair knew that. So, he chose to believe that against all odds, they would come back; that they'd miss him, and would return to take them, up, up and away from here, through the portal, even now was shrinking, dissipating, and disappearing leaving nothing behind but the unreachable, unfathomably vast galaxy above.

Living Bad Dreams
By Denise Hatfield

When dreams come alive, there's no telling where they will lead. Everything changes when you realize that, dream or no dream, you're going to die. What do you do then?

Ordering Link:
Print Edition: https://www.hiraethsffh.com/product-page/living-bad-dreams-by-denise-hatfield-1

ePub edition: https://www.hiraethsffh.com/product-page/living-bad-dreams-by-denise-hatfield-2

Aunt Carol's House
Megan Renee Doyle

I wasn't exactly sure what to include in a ghost-banishing kit, so I just gathered various junk from around my apartment that might help: the flashlight from Dani's toolbox, some salt from the back of my pantry, and the rosary my grandmother gave me for my first Communion.

Maybe crucifixes and salt were better against vampires and demons. I didn't exactly know how to deal with a ghost—I probably should have thought a little more about it before confronting one.

But I let the righteous indignation carry me all the way into my car, down the familiar route, and then parked in the driveway of Aunt Carol's house in the middle of the night.

All the windows were dark. Aunt Carol wasn't home; she wouldn't be back until mid-morning at the earliest. And that's exactly what I needed: her safely out of the way.

I'd be lying if I said I wasn't nervous looking up at that big house. Its steepled rooflines and vacant windows suddenly felt intimidating and imperious. I'd never been there after dark before, and now I was hyper aware of myself. I felt like an interloper in something that was much bigger, older, and more mysterious than myself.

It was a lot to take in, and my heart pounded nervously as I got out of the car.

. . .

I'm always told how much I remind everyone of Aunt Carol. I'm not exactly sure how we're related. I think she's my great-aunt, connected somewhere down the line.

Based on old pictures I've seen, I suppose I have her eyes. Something in the cut of our chins is similar. She spent her whole life unmarried, and I was definitely a disaster in the dating department. But, as far as I've heard, she's more of a loner. An eccentric.

"You both just march to the beats of your own drums," my mother would tactfully say. "She's all alone in that big house, and she's getting on in years."

Mom wanted me to go over and check on her. She said Aunt Carol had broken her phone—apparently she still only used a landline—and needed help mounting it back on the wall so she wouldn't have to bend over to use it.

I said I might if I had time later. Aunt Carol could always hire a real handyperson to help her if she needed it fixed now. Someone who actually knew what they were doing.

"Oh honey, it's not like you have a job right now. You could use the distraction." Harsh. But unfortunately true. I was also pointedly ignoring all texts that didn't come from family. Especially any from Dani.

I rang the doorbell to the old faded Victorian, and chimes sounded somewhere from deep within the house. The sun was high in the sky, and bugs screeched in the surrounding trees.

I clutched the handle to the toolbox, still practically unused since it was gifted to me. I mentally went through the tools I knew and their uses. If my limited knowledge failed me, there were always tutorials on the internet.

Nobody answered. The curtain behind the decoratively cut glass remained firmly shut. She was expecting me, right?

I knocked on the door. Still no answer. I rang the bell —the chimes sounded again—but still nobody came.

I thought about it for a moment. Mom surely told Aunt Carol I was coming. Then again, the woman was also having phone problems.

Hesitantly, I pushed on the door, and it swung inward, creaking on old iron hinges. Inside the house was dark. The thick curtains over every window deepened and distorted every shadow into hungry shapes.

"Hello?" I called, voice shaky with uncertainty. "Aunt Carol?"

I stepped inside. I knew her house was old, but I wasn't prepared for the truly intimidating presence of an authentic Victorian. The house was monstrous, with uneven wooden floors and cramped hallways that closed in from every direction.

"It's me," I said into the oppressive emptiness, "Margie's daughter."

The place had almost no natural light, and her things —while clean and tidy—were old relics from a different time. Stepping into the house was disorienting, as if the very air inside was heavy with something. I just couldn't figure out what.

I gripped the toolbox tightly.

A sudden crash had me jumping nearly out of my skin. The sound was solid and heavy, filled with the jaw-clenching jangle of loose metal.

I froze, hand clutched over my loudly beating heart. Then I followed the noise.

It took two turns before I found myself in a cheerfully cozy kitchen. A small window over the sink let warm sunshine in, and a kettle whistled loudly on the stove. It was a breath of fresh air.

Inside was Aunt Carol, taking the kettle off the heat. She was slightly hunched by age, and she moved stiffly with tight joints. But when she turned and saw me standing in the doorway to her kitchen, she smiled brightly.

Aunt Carol was friendly. She called me things like *sweetie* and *dear*. And when I tried to apologize for barging in on her, she waved it away and said that she must not have heard the doorbell. Then she hugged me tightly. Her cardigan smelled like caramel and mothballs.

I was ready to get straight to work, but Carol said that she made tea first so we could catch up, and would I please "be a dear and get some spoons from that drawer?"

I opened it to look inside, but as soon as I let go of the knob, the whole drawer immediately slid closed again with a clattering crash. It was the same noise I'd heard earlier. Installed at a steep enough angle that it wouldn't stay open.

"Houses as old as these have their charming quirks," Aunt Carol explained.

Mom had made it sound like she was desperately lonely. Maybe she was at least a little bit, considering how much she talked. But Aunt Carol seemed genuinely happy with her big house and her simple life. She had friends at her knitting club. She had her cozy kitchen stuffed with delicious smells and soft fabrics.

Aunt Carol cursed with words like *blazes* and *drat*, which felt anachronistic for her generation, but not for the house she lived in.

She talked a little about the history of the house. How it even went back to 1887 and first housed a three-generation family. She described some of the updates it had had over the decades—things to upgrade it for modern living without compromising its historic charm.

Aunt Carol also asked me about my life. I stalled, not sure how many details Mom had given her. She expressed regret and concern about the layoff. That was fine. A frustrating situation but fine.

"And do you have anyone special in your life?" Her smile was genuine, trying to reach out and get to know me.

Instead, I looked guiltily at the cooling mug of tea between my hands. Do I have anyone special? I wasn't sure anymore.

I quickly gulped down the last of my tea then stood up with purpose. "I should get to work. Point me to where this phone is."

Her smile fell a little, yet the cheerfulness never left her eyes. Thankfully she decided not to press.

Mom had said the phone fell off the mount. I thought maybe the drywall had chipped away and I'd have to rehang the whole thing.

But no. The damage was worse.

The phone mount had been completely torn off, and a chunk of the wall—full-blown hardwood, mind you, not cheap side paneling—had splintered away, leaving a sizeable gouge.

I stared at it dumbly for a solid thirty seconds, trying to calculate exactly how this small old woman could have done this herself.

"It's not too bad, is it?" She looked a little embarrassed.

"I—uh, no. I can rig this until we get the wall fixed."

I was a little clumsy with the tools, but it felt good to work on something with my hands. And, considering the real damage would require an actual carpenter that she would have to hire later, I didn't even have to stop for too many online tutorials. I just needed to make sure the phone could be hung back up securely in a nearby space.

While I worked, Aunt Carol sat with me and chatted; she was happy to take the reins in the conversation. I even found myself opening up and offering tidbits from my childhood. She had wonderful stories about my grandmother. And I gave her silly anecdotes about Mom.

We talked for hours, even after I finished my work, tugging on the phone mount a few times to make sure it was safe and secure. It had been a long time since I'd sat down and actually talked to someone—without one or both of us having to rush to a meeting, finish up some work, or slot in time to run an errand. It felt nice to let time pass at its own pace. And I genuinely enjoyed getting to know Aunt Carol.

I was just letting her know to call me anytime to fix anything else that came up—absolutely no trouble at all, I promise—when a crash from the kitchen startled us both into silence.

It was the utensil door slamming closed.

I swallowed nervously, not sure what to say. How on earth did the utensil drawer suddenly shut? It couldn't have been open on its own.

But Aunt Carol chuckled nervously and glanced at the clock on the mantelpiece. "It's getting late. I don't want to keep you."

I indicated toward the kitchen. "Is someone—?"

"Oh no," she interrupted me cheerfully. "Old houses, you know."

I looked at the gouge in the wall where her phone used to hang. Right. Old houses.

Aunt Carol hustled me out of the house after that, albeit with profuse thanks and compliments on my work. Before I knew it, I was back in my car and driving away. The silhouette of Aunt Carol's house watched over me from the rearview mirror, growing darker and sharper in the lengthening shadows of the sunset.

. . .

As days turned into weeks and I still had no luck finding a job, Mom continued sending me to go fix things at Aunt Carol's house. Of course, I was happy to see her again. I even started looking up DIY tutorials when I had free time.

While I worked, she talked, and I listened. When I started adding my own commentary, she would laugh so hard that her whole body would shake with the joy of it. It felt good, blooming in the glow of her laughter.

Maybe I had been getting lonely too.

In between her stories, I started telling her about me. I vented my frustrations about not finding anything better than short-term contract work and the absolute hellscape job hunting was. I relayed my worries about my career. How it felt like I had stalled with no way to go up or improve my skills. Faced with an endless and long-winded shuffle of dissatisfaction. Even as I hustled and moved and exhausted myself, I was never progressing, so it always felt like I was standing still.

I was always happy to visit Aunt Carol's house. However, no matter what I fixed, there was always new damage with no explanation.

A whole tree branch fell in her backyard, even though there was no bad storm and the tree was still healthy and strong. I chopped it up and hauled the pieces to the front curb to be taken away.

All the chairs in the dining room had their legs broken off one night. I cleaned up the mess and assembled some quick replacements.

A window was smashed, and I found someone to install a new one. She claimed it was just some neighborhood children, but her house was on a half-hidden lot at the back of an old neighborhood, and I never spotted any kids nearby.

The repeated destruction baffled me. I mentioned some of my worries to Mom. It wasn't like the house was falling down around her, but it didn't seem entirely safe either.

Mom jokingly replied, "Maybe her house is haunted."

. . .

One of the stairs to her basement collapsed, which was just complicated enough to test my new skills. I did the best I could, crouched over the rough stairs. As usual, Aunt Carol sat on the top step, talking to me while I worked.

She was talking about a friend of hers. I couldn't remember if she'd said they met in knitting club; I knew her name was Eugenie, because it struck me as an old-fashioned name, even for Aunt Carol's generation. She talked about Eugenie tenderly—shy smile on her face even as her eyes seemed to stare off into the middle distance—so maybe they were a little something more than friends.

Maybe it was the peaceful look on Aunt Carol's face when she talked about Eugenie. Maybe it was the weeks of companionship we'd shared when we were both at least a little bit lonely. But I finally decided to tell Aunt Carol about Dani.

Dani had wanted to move in with me, even after I had lost my job. She'd given me the toolbox because she wanted us to build a life together. However, I couldn't offer what she truly wanted. It was hard to say it out loud, but it was also a relief to tell someone. I hadn't even given Mom the entire story.

"Then what happened?" Aunt Carol asked, sincere eyes dark with understanding.

"Then we broke up," I said, voice small. Dani wouldn't admit it, but I knew it was just like me and my career. She was desperate to move our relationship in a direction—any direction. But while she was rowing the canoe, I had dropped my paddle. Or I never really had one. We were going in circles. Spinning out. Getting tired. Going nowhere fast.

Dani had given up calling me weeks ago, but she still sent texts. She thought we could work through this. But I already knew it wasn't enough. I would never be enough for her.

"Sometimes," Carol said, absently lost in thought, "when we're worried about losing something, we grip on too tight . . . or we toss it as far away from us as we can so it that maybe it hurts less when it's gone. Either way, we end up breaking things instead."

"Even if it's completely unfixable in the first place?"

And then a crash. From somewhere deep inside the house. The utensil drawer had slammed closed again.

"Was that—?" I started to say.

"Old houses, dear." She stood up, looking back and forth between me and the direction of the kitchen. "I'll go make sure everything's okay. I'm sure it's fine, though."

I moved to follow her, but she insisted that I should stay. I could keep working. Then she left me alone on the broken stairs to the basement.

Aunt Carol insisted it was nothing, but I couldn't help but think about Mom's words. *Maybe her house is haunted.*

No, that's ridiculous. I turned back to my work, picking up the hammer again, when the sound of soft skittering echoed from the basement below. *What the hell was that?* There were no lights on below, so it was too dark to see.

It was probably fine. Although, if Aunt Carol had rats, I would need to call an exterminator before I left.

Then, another sound came from below. A gentle yet persistent creak of a human body stepping on old wood. That was no rat.

"Hello?" I called uneasily. The door to the rest of the house was open, and I had the warm lightbulb over the stairs plus the flashlight to help me see the repair. They did very little to cut into the gloom below.

There was another long, slow creak. Closer this time.

I stood up, unsure whether to creep forward and find out what the noise was or retreat into the relative safety of the proper house. I tried my hardest to peer into the darkness, but I couldn't see much more than the vague outlines of boxes and covered furniture. I didn't hear the sound again.

This was stupid. I was getting worked up over nothing, and I needed to get back to my work anyway. Aunt Carol would send me home soon.

I reached into the toolbox . . . and caught a glance of something behind me.

I stumbled back, a half-garbled scream caught in my throat. In my blind haste, I mis-stepped and then had the stomach-churning sensation of stepping into midair before I fell the last couple steps and landed hard on my butt. The leveling tool clattered down each step with me.

"What's wrong?" Aunt Carol called out.

I could hear her footsteps cross the floor above me, coming straight for the top of the stairs, then she appeared, pale face anxious. "Are you hurt?"

I shakily rose to my feet. "No, I'm fine. Just a little tumble."

I didn't tell her, though, why I fell. I'd looked behind me just a moment, but I was sure I saw it. A woman had been standing on the basement steps, between me and the door to the first floor. It wasn't Aunt Carol. But then, who else could it have been?

Aunt Carol hurried me out of the house after that. I'd have to come back to finish fixing the step. It was way too late. I tried to protest that I was fine. It was just a clumsy moment. But she would hear none of it.

I numbly gathered my things and made it to my car without protest. Then, as Carol was closing the front door, I saw her again.

This time, in one of the upstairs windows—I'm pretty sure it was Aunt Carol's bedroom—I saw her silhouette. That strange woman I'd seen in the basement. Her shape was clear and stark against the light of the room behind it, especially in the gathering darkness of the sunset.

That's when I realized. Aunt Carol always hurried me out of the house by a certain time, no matter what. She always welcomed me with open arms during the day.

But I don't think I'd ever been in her house at night.

. . .

I let myself in, using my flashlight to help guide me in the late-night darkness. Fingers never far from where the rosary sat in my pocket. I'd been coming by to fix things so often lately that Aunt Carol had given me a key.

The house was dark and silent . . . ominously so. But it also seemed to thrum alive with my arrival, as if to wake up specifically to greet me.

I called out an uneasy hello, half expecting something to answer back. But the house swallowed the sound of my voice.

Automatically, my feet guided me to the kitchen, like I would go to greet Aunt Carol as usual. But it wasn't daytime, and Aunt Carol wasn't here.

I entered the kitchen and turned on the overhead light, harsh and blinding after the oppressive darkness. My stomach felt unsettled at the sight of every cabinet and drawer wide open. Carol kept things neat; she didn't leave the house like this.

Even the utensil drawer—just like every other drawer in the room—was stuck open, stretched anxiously taught by some invisible force.

I was morbidly curious, even though I knew it was probably a bad idea. With nervous fingers, I pushed against the drawer. It didn't take much pressure to close it. My fingers easily guided it back closed, although not as quickly as if it had been taken by gravity.

When it slid shut, it was like some invisible wire had been snipped, and immediately every cabinet door and drawer swung back to its natural force of gravity, whether completely closed or wider open. I jumped at all the movement, heart lodged in my throat. But it was like the whole kitchen released a breath of relief. The tension in the room eased. The silence in here was natural again.

The air around me no longer felt as electrically charged, but if anything, I felt more nervous than ever. This wasn't natural. Something had been holding the drawers and cabinets open. Even if whatever it was had fled further into the house, I had no doubt it was still here.

Then, there was noise overhead. As I looked up at the ceiling and tracked the steady sound of human footfalls on the floor above, I believed that my theory was holding more and more weight.

. . .

One day, I had to help Aunt Carol hang up all the photos in the parlor. Apparently they had just fallen off the wall.

When I arrived, I realized that she'd downplayed the damage. Every frame was broken, and smashed pieces of glass littered the floor. I glanced at some of the shelving and knickknacks elsewhere in the room. Nothing else was touched . . . or looked even the smallest bit askew. Yet every hanging photograph had been yanked down and broken.

It took a few afternoons to get that mess back to the way it was. I cleaned the fragments and shards right away, of course, but there were dozens of photos hanging collage-style around that room, and they all needed new frames.

They went back decades. Some photos were colorful family shots from recent years. Some had the washed-out colors of decades past. I even recognized one of Mom from when she was a teenager.

Many were black-and-white photos from deep in the past. In prime placement was probably the oldest. Instead of some relative I barely recognized, it was a woman standing in front of Aunt Carol's house.

Only, the house looked new—with clean, crisp lines on gables that were now weathered with age, and I could see the unmistakable texture of bare wood beams in a half-constructed roof.

She held her head high, jutting her chin playfully in the direction of the camera. Arms crossed regally in front of her high-necked dress.

Something about her expression was imperious and alluring. I found myself staring transfixed.

"Beautiful, isn't she?" I hadn't even heard Aunt Carol coming up behind me. She beamed with pride.

I swallowed nervously. She was beautiful. I couldn't deny that. But I had seen this woman before, and it wasn't in this photograph. She'd been standing on the basement steps. She'd been watching out the upstairs window. Aunt Carol lived alone, and this woman was clearly from a hundred and fifty years ago.

It sounded crazy in my head, but I had only one explanation that could be true. The only question was, how do you say that you think you've seen a ghost?

"Was she a relative?" I asked.

Aunt Carol chuckled. "Oh no. Definitely not." And that's all she offered before thanking me profusely for my work and sending me on my way.

It was almost getting dark, after all.

That night I researched everything I could find online about Aunt Carol's house and any and all rumors of ghosts. But, unlike in the movies, there was nothing sensational to pick up. Aunt Carol had lived there, happily and quietly, since she was a young woman, and as far as I could tell, so had the family before her. I couldn't even figure out the name of that woman in the photo.

I knew I had seen her inside that house, though—as impossible as that seemed. Plus, after following a rabbit hole into descriptions of poltergeists and reflecting on all the recent damage that Aunt Carol's house had sustained, I couldn't help but come to one conclusion. Aunt Carol certainly wasn't damaging her own things. But why didn't she say something?

I wish I'd seen the pattern before Mom called me that night.

I had hung up the phone on her before I could fully process everything. All I knew was that Aunt Carol had gone to the hospital. Something about falling and breaking her leg . . . or maybe it was her foot. I blinked back the tears and instead chose to focus all the rushing blood in my face on my rising anger.

I was sure of it. Aunt Carol's house was haunted by the woman who used to live there. And she probably hurt her tonight.

Aunt Carol wouldn't be home. I had that thought before I leapt into action, grabbing my keys and whatever else I thought might help. Then I jumped into my car with barely the semblance of a half-baked plan. Flashlight, salt, and rosary.

. . .

So now here I was, listening to steady human footfalls on the floor above and wishing I'd come to the house with more than a fiery determination for justice.

The ghost was here. Upstairs. Probably near the master bedroom. She'd hurt Aunt Carol, and I had no idea how to deal with her. But I had to try.

I took the stairs slowly, wincing at every creak in the old floorboards. Despite my best efforts to be stealthy, the footsteps on the floor above followed my progress. The woman—the ghost—whoever it was—circled in an antsy arc on the floor above. As my steps up the stairs took me toward the second-floor landing, those ominous steps matched me. Inch by inch. Moving closer to each other.

It was a long way down back to the first floor, and I couldn't help but picture Aunt Carol, an old woman walking confidently in her own home, up bare wooden steps. What if she was pushed down the stairs? How would she have felt, plummeting into midair, as time slowed down and the rough stairs rushed up from below?

It made me dizzy just thinking about it, and I knew I had to harden my resolve. Instead of giving in to the fear, I rushed the last few steps, running as quickly as I could, courage screwed tight and held somewhere firmly in my belly.

I burst onto the second-floor landing and almost ran right into a wall.

I was scared. Oh my god, I was so scared. But I let the adrenaline take over, and as I whipped around, ready to fight off any ghostly presence, I realized that there was no one there. No mysterious woman. Nothing at all.

"Where are you, you coward?"

Only the silence of the empty house met me.

"Fucking fight me!"

It took a beat, and then I flinched as the sound of something heavy crashed downstairs—louder than the utensil drawer in the kitchen. In the immediate aftermath of the noise, I swore I could hear the telltale scrape of splintering wood.

She must've been downstairs now.

I froze. The fear pushed back up to the surface, and I could feel my legs quiver beneath me. I shouldn't have come here. Not alone. Not after dark. I wanted to run. I wanted to fight. I wanted to sink into the floor and curl up into a ball until my mom could come and rescue me.

But then, after a few seconds of sheer terror in the wake of the crash, a new noise wafted up from downstairs. It was faint, but I could just make it out. Fast and rhythmic tonal beeping. The unmistakable sound of a phone left too long off the hook.

That brought me back to my senses. This woman had torn Aunt Carol's phone off the wall again. It was the first repair I made for her. The first sign that all was not right at her house.

I pulled out my rosary beads and went downstairs. This time I didn't care if she could hear me coming. I let my anger take me all the way to where the phone lay on the floor of the parlor. Handset scattered away from the base, beeping monotonously into the stale darkness.

Standing there, swallowed by the deep shadows inside the parlor, was the woman. I could barely make out her transparent silhouette, if it weren't for a small bit of movement. The gentle billow of her skirts, moved by an unfelt breeze.

The ghost—the woman—looked so much like her portrait in the parlor, but while she'd been young and precocious, challenging the world around her to dare try and hold her back, now she was older, face bearing the lines of middle age. She looked very real, occupying space in this old house that truly fit her.

But I could also tell that she was marked by death. Her cheeks were sunken with sickness, and the dark circles under her eyes had an especially bruised look, more extreme than mere sleeplessness. She'd been pale in that black-and-white photograph, but something about the shades of green in her dress really highlighted the hauntingly unnatural pallor of her face. She truly looked like a corpse recently risen from peaceful rest.

She was pitifully other. She was a terrifying reminder of mortality. Yet, she was also beautiful.

She stared straight at me. "Where is she?" Her voice was surprisingly soft.

I hesitated, fear and anger warring within me. Here I was, in my great-aunt's Victorian house, confronting a ghost. And she had the gall to demand where the victim of her haunting was. It was ridiculous, and I didn't know whether to burst out laughing or let out a sob.

I raised my grandmother's rosary with more confidence than I felt.

It didn't faze her. "*Where is she?*" She put more force into her voice, and the air seemed to reverberate. A nearby side table flipped over, causing the lamp on top of it to shatter and several knickknacks to tumble across the rug.

A small framed photo of Aunt Carol flew at me, and I barely ducked out of the way. I dropped the rosary and instead brandished the flashlight, holding it in a two-handed grip like a baseball bat. I hopped out of the way of scattered glass. The extra shot of adrenaline let me clasp tight onto my simmering anger.

"She's not here. Haven't you done enough?" My voice was shaking, but it quickly became stronger as I built up my momentum. "Congrats, you win. You get your house back or whatever."

She looked upset; I had no idea why. "I don't want her gone," she said.

"Then what?" I demanded. "Do you want to hurt her bad enough that she dies too?" The thought pulled something ugly and tight within me.

"No!" Her shoulders shook.

"You hurt her. She's in the hospital because of you." I poured the past several weeks of worry and uncertainty and concern and helplessness into my words. "She was here all alone while you terrorized her."

I was crying now. This wasn't how it was supposed to go. I needed to stay strong in front of this threat. I needed to stay strong so I could defend Aunt Carol.

I continued yelling my frustrated feelings out at the ghost. Why did Aunt Carol have to deal with this all alone? Why didn't she ask for help, even when I was there almost every day? Why didn't she get herself out? Why did she continue, even as things got worse and worse? Why didn't she leave? I vented until my voice gave out, breathing heavily. Exhausted.

The ghost was weeping. We both were. We both stood there, in Aunt Carol's house, in the middle of the night, sobbing with pent-up emotions that had been released all at once, too big to hold inside anymore.

And that's when Aunt Carol finally came home. "Oh my." That's all she said when she saw us—the ghost and me —crying in her living room. The only sign of injury was the support boot on her right leg.

She hobbled forward, and to my surprise, she went straight toward the ghost, who was still crying, face hidden in her hands and shoulders shaking with each hitch and sob.

"It's okay, my darling. I'm here." Carol's arms carefully encircled the ghost's. She hovered over her but did not touch her—I imagined if she had, she might have gone straight through. Carol hummed a soft and soothing tune as she bent close to the woman, and the woman slowed her cries, leaning in toward Carol as if there was a gentle magnetic pull between them.

I felt a piece of the loneliness in my own heart pull. I ached in the sad comfort in its glow. It was completely unexpected yet at the same time somehow familiar.

Then something clicked into place. These soft words of comfort. Aunt Carol's refusal to deal with her house's haunting. Her lack of discernible loneliness despite being so often alone. A soft and proud smile when she brought up her friend Eugenie, with the old-fashioned name.

These women *knew* each other—for a long time, I guessed. Their relationship was clearly more tender than two people who happened to occupy the same house.

When Aunt Carol finished calming down the ghost, she was finally ready to tell me everything.

I wanted answers, but I no longer demanded them. The tears, the adrenaline, the fear, and the late hour had caught up to me, and I was tired. But I also refused to leave until my worries were laid to rest.

Aunt Carol hadn't fallen down the stairs. And Eugenie—the ghost—hadn't caused her accident. She'd tripped at the grocery store, and it had taken time to get her foot set.

Aunt Carol and the ghost had been *companions* for a long time now—that's what Eugenie called them.

"And you don't want to hurt her?" I asked. "Even if she could be—well—a ghost too?"

Eugenie hesitated. "I don't know how or why I am here, honestly. There are no guarantees. And I won't risk that I may never see her again." She looked to Aunt Carol, distress clear on her face. "And yet I know it will happen. Soon, even." She held up a transparent hand, barely hovering over Aunt Carol's wrinkled cheek. "My love, I'm so sorry for everything I've done."

"Hush now, we've gone over this." Carol moved closer toward Eugenie, both caught into each other's orbit. To me, she explained, "These are powers we're not meant to understand. Sometimes regret and worry manifest physically."

She turned back to Eugenie. "And they're only objects."

Regret and worry. It made sense. Sometimes, when we worry that we'll lose something, we'll hold on too tight. Or we'll cast it away hoping it would hurt less without it. Either way, something will break. Eugenie was clearly unable to let go.

Aunt Carol was no longer a young woman. A minor fall had sent her to the hospital. I'd only known her for several weeks, and I loved her so fiercely that I'd stormed a haunted house for her. My fear and concern for her well-being had been so visceral. But now, in the aftermath of that fear, there was still a seedling of worry.

We all die eventually, don't we? It's the most natural thing in the world. Yet I couldn't help the gut-churning sense of dread at the thought of losing Aunt Carol. Mom had been right. Aunt Carol and I were similar. I would feel so much more alone without her.

I thought of Dani. I'd left her so callously. All because I was afraid of what might happen between us. The relationship that Aunt Carol and Eugenie had was so tender, so devoted. Yet it was fragile. A relationship stalled. They were already separated by death. They had never truly been together, had they?

"It's sad, isn't it?"

Aunt Carol gave me one of her patented warm smiles of sheer happiness and hugged me. She knew what I was talking about. "No, dear," she said. "We've shared quiet moments and major events together. We've been with each other through better and worse. We've been each other's confidantes and sources of joy. We've had a whole life together."

There are no guarantees. In life or death. There's no way to make sure we will always be together, and there's no telling what will happen to us.

But isn't that true of everyone we love? There's no use fretting when we should be enjoying the limited time we do have—to its fullest extent. With or without physical intimacy. In any way that makes sense for us. And I knew—deep in my heart—*that* was the truth.

Aunt Carol made me promise, should ever happen to her—if she couldn't make her way back—that I'd make sure Eugenie wouldn't be lonely. I swore to her, and I meant it.

We stayed up the rest of the night. Me, Aunt Carol, and the ghost Eugenie. Just talking. Getting to know each other. Sharing our secrets, our fears, and our hopes.

Then, in the morning, I finally called Dani.

The Oculist's Daughter
By Angel Favazza

The Oculist's Daughter by Angel Favazza is a steampunker in the old west. It's got a semi-mad scientist (her dad), her, of course, plus outlaws, Indians, Wyoming, a poison gas for killing natives, and an Indian guide. It all adds up to a rollicking adventure.

https://www.hiraethsffh.com/product-page/oculist-s-daughter-by-angel-favazza

Wayang Kulit
Richard E. Schell

In Java, the indigenous people celebrate their religion through elaborate stories that have been told for generations, using shadow puppets against an opaque screen illuminated by fire. According to their shaman, the plays tell stories of the dream world, which the people believe is just as real as the world of the awakened. The puppet ceremonies are called Wayang Kulit.

I work for a multinational import-export business where many of our products are manufactured in Southeast Asia by our several business partners. My work requires lots of travel, but I enjoy the contrast of experiencing different cultures, food, and historical sites.

Our overseas contacts work in towering modern plants, but during my time off, I always enjoy historical sites, temples, and the local street markets. The markets especially fascinate with their exotic foods, spices, and traditional medicine   shops.
One day, I entered a particularly intriguing herbal medicine shop. Its doors were so ancient and recessed that they could be easily overlooked. Walking by, I was almost unaware of its existence. I was mesmerized by the elderly shopkeeper who, despite her age, seemed to float across the room with unlimited strength and grace.

I was surprised when she calmly said in her broken English, "I was expecting you. I have what you seek."

I jokingly said, "I would like to get whatever you are taking."

"Yes, but I know truly that this is what you require because she has chosen you. However, I must warn you that this medicine is powerful. It comes from Java, where their world is very different than what you are used to, Remember, this treatment works in the other world, not this world, the world of dreams. She is a fickle mistress, and cross her at your peril".

I happily paid for the herbal medication and left curious about what benefits I might experience. I completed all my shopping and errands and anxiously headed back to my hotel, as I had some important negotiations the following morning with one of our potential manufacturers.

I took the tea according to her instructions but did not feel any changes. Because of the meeting the next day, I went to bed early. During that night, I had the most vivid dream of my life. In that dream, I entered the pharmacy with the same shopkeeper who took me to the far back of her dispensary to a door, where she asked me to enter.

Upon entering, I found myself in a conference room filled with the management team of our overseas manufacturer. During the negotiations, they proposed that I write my best and final offer, which they would accept or reject based on meeting their minimal acceptable standards. In the dream, I proposed what I thought was an unacceptable low bid. I suddenly awoke from my dream, still focused on every detail I could remember.

Early the next day I met our manufacturing partners to complete the negotiations for production of our new products.

"We have enjoyed our long relationship with your company. However, regarding negotiating a price, we have been unable to come to mutually agreeable terms with your management on this project. We greatly appreciate the time you took to meet us here in person and share with us your financial constraints."

"We would like to propose the following means to complete our negotiations in the most mutually beneficial and timely manner. We will write down the minimum amount that we will be able to manufacture your products. If your offer is above our minimum, we will accept your contract if it is not, we will respectfully decline. You are then free to negotiate your best price with any of our competitors who can serve your needs. Please use this opportunity to give your best and final offer. I hope we can look forward to a long, synergistic relationship in the years to come."

I then proposed the exact monetary amount I had in my dream. The manufacturing suppliers' surprise was palpable as they pulled out their cost analysis paperwork, revealing the same bid amount as the pre-agreed minimum they would accept. I was complimented on my analysis and skill in facilitating a final contract, even if they had hoped for more favorable terms. My company was also thrilled to have negotiations completed with an agreement saving them more than they had counted on.

I continued taking the herbal formula nightly before bed. A few nights later, I had another vivid dream. In it, I walked through the herbalist's back door as I had in the previous dream. Upon entering the door, I saw myself speaking to the airline representative while rescheduling my flight for two days later than I originally planned to return home.

The following day, I rescheduled my flight as I had my dream. Calling my wife that evening, I told her that plans changed and I would be arriving two days later than scheduled. She asked why I had changed plans on such short notice. Embarrassed and wishing to avoid an explanation of the real reason, I told her I still had work to iron out with our negotiations, which would require a few more days.

I decided to use my few remaining days to explore sites away from the usual tourist destinations. I explored exotic ruins of shrines set amongst the most beautiful countryside and farmlands unchanged for decades or centuries. While on my excursion, I got a phone call from my wife asking if I had watched the news. I explained that I had been away from my hotel all day without outside contact. She explained that the same flight I had previously scheduled, had a malfunction on the runway, and several people were seriously injured. The strange coincidence of my dream and the plane crash began haunting my thoughts night and day.

That night, I experienced another vivid dream. Similar to the others, it started with me entering the pharmacy's back door. Entering, I found myself in my hotel room speaking to my brother Frank on the telephone. He and I were involved in finalizing discussions about an investment in which 1 committed to join him. This scene seemed particularly out of character to me because, over the years, my wife and I had several bad experiences with his business dealings. We committed never to be involved in them again.

As expected, my wife June called the following morning to tell me that Frank had called and asked when I would be back as he wanted to talk to me about an opportunity. She was emphatic that we not get involved in any more of his "dubious schemes" ever again.

Sure enough, later that day, Frank called and wanted to discuss his latest investment proposal and hoped we would join him in it. Usually, this involved fronting him money to participate. He was markedly upset when I told him that June and I would not be participating with him this time. I explained that we wished him well and that I needed to respect June's wishes. I had an unexplainable dread, knowing that I had not fulfilled my dream's destiny.

As the last of my supply of herbs dwindled, I had another remarkable dream. In it, I again entered the pharmacist's back door. I found myself walking on the street market, heading down the now familiar path toward the shop. As I awakened, I struggled to grasp an interpretation of the dream before its details blurred from my memory. My best explanation was that I was to return to the shop. I decided to head back to the market and purchase a supply of the tea before flying home the following evening.

In the morning, I got up early and packed my luggage to be well-prepared for the flight that evening. I then headed to the same street market toward the traditional herbalist's shop, compelled by my recent dream. As I walked down the street, I realized I must have passed it, distracted by crowds and the many unusual events of my trip. In doubling back, I became perplexed by my inability to find the recessed storefront. I began asking a number of the other shopkeepers for directions, but no one seemed to have any recollection of the shop or the remarkable elderly pharmacist who owned it. One shopkeeper insisted that he had been coming to work on the same street every day for over 25 years and had never seen the herbalist shop I described. After hours of walking back and forth, I gave up searching for the herbalist and her shop in the narrow recesses of the crowded market and returned to the hotel to collect my baggage for my long flight home.

From the mind of K. S. Hardy . . .

The tales of K. S. Hardy blend Grimm and Poe in a heady mix of dark and strange. From "Sometimes Above the Trees" to "The Snake's Defense," and all points in between, Hardy takes you on a tour through the unexpected and the inexplicable. Have a seat, put your feet up . . . and leave all the lights on.

https://www.hiraethsffh.com/product-page/weaving-the-light-by-k-s-hardy

Robes
Laurel Hanson

Zadab had seen plenty of dead slaves before, but never a dead nobleman. The man looked small and insignificant in the bright puddle of his silks— orange, yellow, purple—the *bandeem* still covering his face.

When Mistress Sarroway had called for him to join the search for the missing man, he'd been down in the well since long before the first cock crow, dreaming of flat bread and honey cakes as he turned the treadwheel. Her call of, "Zadab-ab-ab-ab-" had volleyed down the stone walls, like the mournful wail of sand ghosts.

"Madam, I hear you!" he shouted. "You-you-you" bounced upwards to the mouth of the well, which appeared to Zadab as a bowl full of fading stars. Now and then, thin ribbons of firelight flickered across it.

The wheel silenced when he leapt off, and then moaned sadly as the weight of the full buckets settled back into the water. He'd have to haul them up all over again, but his nineteen years had taught him that failure to respond to her summons swiftly would earn him another beating. He raced up the steps that spiraled around the sides of the well, the worn scoops of stone smooth beneath his bare feet.

Even before he mounted the wall at the top, Mistress Sarroway was shouting her demand. "Master Chaleem has wandered away from the caravan and must be found or they lose the day's travel." Around her, the courtyard of the caravanserai boiled with activity. Everywhere, voices called out, "Master Chaleem!" and torches were thrust like swords into pre-dawn shadows. Donkeys brayed in agitation while the saddled camels placidly steamed their wet breath with a disdainful air at the hurrying figures.

Mistress Sarroway ran her caravanserai with a tight fist. A missing nobleman would cause a scandal up and down the trade route, which explained the pinched anger knotting her face. She gripped the arm of a slave boy who looked a few years younger than Zadab and a good deal more frightened. Thrusting both the boy and the torch at him, she snapped, "Take this one and search the springways. Master Chaleem must be found."

The last place a nobleman *should* be found, was down in the springways, Zadab thought, but bowed briefly to show his understanding. He jerked his head for the lad to follow him back into the well.

On the third step, the lad hesitated, staring wide-eyed into the depths where the river gleamed, a dark mirror reflecting starlight. To fall into it, Zadab had often thought, would be an endless flight into a night sky. He found the idea comforting but knew the lad saw only the very long fall. Most people were the same; their muscles would harden in fear while their minds would tempt them towards that flightless plunge.

He patted the lad's shoulder before resuming his descent into a darkness only made blacker by the light of the torch. "Why do you think your master is in the springways?"

"Because he's nowhere else and your mistress has commanded." Mustaar's voice trembled as violently as his hand gripping the back of Zadab's tunic. "What's a springway?"

"The underground river brings water for the caravanserai," Zadab explained. "In the spring, runoff from the mountains of the Noose floods the river and it rises to fill the tunnels higher up. The springways." He loved that time of the year as then he didn't have to haul the water so far.

He slipped into the first tunnel, his torch throwing its light uneasily into the narrow space. "I don't see why he would be in here. They say if you get lost in the springways, only the springflood will find you to flush out your corpse."

"Master Chaleem would often seek solitary places for some purpose of his own. He does things I don't understand." The boy must have hit his head because he let out a string of profanity involving dogs and Master Chaleem's mother before continuing. "He only just bought me in Salazar's Gate when he joined the caravan. I've never even seen his face. He wears the *bandeem* always."

Zadab didn't think that mattered much. If they found anyone in the tunnels, it would surely be the missing man. No one else ever entered them except him. He often hid there to avoid his mistress' tempers and had long grown comfortable in the lightless silence.

"I don't think he's a good man," Mustaar added. "He talked only of some essence he thought to find in the mountains of the Noose. I think that's what he said, anyway. He spoke strangely. Not like a Zandimyn. Like a foreigner."

Foreigner or not, when they found the man, he was most definitely dead. Zadab lifted the *bandeem,* the netted face cloth worn for protection from the desert sun. Eyes the color of lapis lazuli stared up at them, glinting in the torchlight. He hissed and spat swiftly to the side to ward off evil, though why the dead nobleman should make him think of evil, he couldn't have said.

The blue-eyed stare seemed so alive, he held the back of his hand to the man's nostrils to be sure. For a moment, he thought he felt a cold breath brush his knuckles, an icy shadow that sent a current of dread jittering into his heart. But then there was nothing. Hastily, he closed the bright stare with his calloused fingers. "Deader than a snakeskin."

Mustaar's nervousness was draining out of him like water from a gourd and replaced with a calculating craftiness. He began pawing at the nobleman's belt, eventually pulling free a plump bag. "He won't be needing coin where he's gone to."

A part of Zadab wanted to protest that robbing the dead might bring a curse upon them, but another part of him felt that he, slave to Mistress Sarroway, had been robbed of his life while he still lived it. Surely that was worse than robbing the dead, yet Mistress Sarroway hadn't suffered from any curses. He held out his palm. "Half," he said.

As the boy began counting the coin, Zadab scanned the tunnel floor but saw no sign of the nobleman's torch. If Master Chaleem had lost his flame in this place, he had likely died of fright. *But what was the man doing in the springways? Besides being dead.*

Mustaar stopped counting to watch Zadab narrowly. "You're almost the same size as my Master Chaleem." When Zadab simply stared back at him, Mustaar added, "You want your freedom?"

Does the moon want the sun? Does a camel want the water? Zadab didn't bother to answer.

Mustaar tossed a sharp glance over his shoulder as if the corpse might be listening. "Become the man," he said. "No one knew Master Chaleem. He didn't join the others at the fires. He just sat alone and wrote in a book. And he never took off the *bandeem*."

"The ways of the nobles are strange," Zadab offered.

The boy rolled his eyes. "No one would know if it was you in his robes. I'll tell the Mistress Sarroway I found you, I mean him, wandering in the springways. The caravan is anxious to depart. They won't care to look closely." When Zadab didn't answer, he added, "I'll say we got separated and you're still in these tunnels. We'll be gone with the caravan before your mistress notices you're missing."

Zadab wasn't used to making decisions for himself but the lad's urgency pressed against him. The caravan awaited its missing nobleman, the drovers, travelers, and merchants impatient to resume their journey. Even the beasts of burden, the camels and horses and donkeys, would be eager to depart in the cool before dawn. And most of all, if the nobleman was not found, Mistress Sarroway's anger would be meted out upon all the slaves who toiled in her caravanserai, himself included. His brain felt like a mouse running in a jar. He wasn't even sure he nodded his agreement, but suddenly Mustaar was stripping the robes from his master, hissing for Zadab's help.

They both fell back on their heels when they pulled the undertunic from the corpse and saw the beaten copper band at the man's neck. "A mage torque!" Mustaar spat to the side. Zadab had never seen a mage, though he'd heard they possessed great powers to aid those who could pay for their services. They could sweeten wells, the stories said, and heal the sick or forecast storms, or even plant thoughts in a person's mind. So too, they could curse the unlucky.

Magecraft was not something for two slaves to meddle with, nor for the likes of a nobleman such as Master Chaleem. He sought out Mustaar's wide eyes for explanation. "Why would your master have such a thing?"

Mustaar shook his head vigorously as though to assure Zadab it was none of his doing.

For a moment, uncertainty reigned in their silence. Then, of their own accord, Zadab's fingers reached out to touch the burnished metal, hesitating only when Mustaar snapped, "Don't touch it!"

"We must take this as well." Zadab's voice shook, but somehow, his fingers moved with a deft confidence to unclasp the torque and slip it around his own neck. His heart hammered at his audacity, and yet a soothing warmth seemed to fill his chest.

Mustaar gave him a surprised nod, freighted with a glimmer of respect. "Good idea. It may be that we can sell such a thing. Hide it beneath his undertunic."

Zadab did so, reveling in the softness of the garment, which slid like air over his scarred shoulders. He struggled with the nobleman's silks, though, his fingers clumsy with the strange folds. When he poked himself for the second time with the ornate pin, he drew bright beads of blood. Mustaar finally rose to help him, and then waited impatiently while Zadab squeezed his splay-toed feet into the narrow, embroidered boots. *How could a man walk in such confinement?*

They pulled Zadab's brown tunic onto the dead man's body, a body so unhardened, Zadab found it hard to credit such a man existed in the world. "No one would mistake him for a slave," he pointed out.

"They will if he's had a chance to rot first. And if they think it's you, then you're dead. To be dead is to be free."

Zadab wasn't sure whether he found Mustaar terribly clever or terribly hard, but he didn't have a chance to sort it out before the idea of freedom filled his mind. He didn't know anything about being free, but it was as if his own body could taste the possibility dangled before him, and it began moving without his instruction. He helped Mustaar drag the nobleman's body to a fissure in the tunnel floor to send it plummeting over. They listened to its meaty thumps as it descended and finally squelched to a stop.

"Stand tall and don't look anyone straight in the eye," Mustaar hissed at him. When Zadab bowed his acknowledgment, Mustaar rolled his eyes again and said, "By the sun and the stars, don't bow to anyone. And pull down the *bandeem* before you are seen. Your eyes are black as the night."

When they returned to the courtyard, Mistress Sarroway harangued Mustaar for taking so long while somehow pouring honey into Zadab's ear at the same time. She hoped "Master Chaleem hadn't been too frightened in the springways." Zadab bobbed his head and felt Mustaar's elbow in his side, warning him to stand straight. He tried, but to stand upright before his mistress made his knees shake. His robes were probably shivering all the way down to his pinched toes from his trembling, but Mistress Sarroway only beamed her relief and whistled for the caravan to depart.

All his life, Zadab had watched the travelers flow out the gates of the caravanserai like a river. He couldn't imagine such freedom. Now, the open gates swam before his eyes. Mustaar had to prod him to mount Master Chaleem's camel and Zadab only just managed to hurl himself into the high saddle before the beast lurched to her feet, pitching him forward and then back again. It was all he could do not to fall off, or worse, cry out in fear.

But then, for the first time in all his years, Zadab rose above those around him. It caught his breath, to look down like a lord upon the heads of the drovers and slaves stewing about the long train of the caravan. He could even look down upon Mistress Sarroway and noticed that the tight coil of her hair was coming undone. He almost smiled.

Mustaar tipped his own smile up at him, a crescent moon catching the rising light. "Very good, Master Chaleem!" he shouted. As the camel began her stately stroll at the heel of the caravan, the lad matched her stride, clucking his tongue encouragingly. Occasionally, he shouted up, "All is well, Master Chaleem. All is well!" as though to be sure his dead master's name was heard up and down the caravan.

They passed through the gates under the paling sky. Zadab thought his chest might explode when he heard "Zadab-ab-ab" at his back. His mistress was calling down the well. How long before she sent someone after her missing slave?

By the time the sun showed over the dunes, he could think of nothing but the clotted air inside the *bandeem*, too thick to breathe. As the sun mounted the sky, turning its soft blues to ash, Zadab no longer considered his fear or his breath, remembering only the dark, cool well he'd left behind.

At mid-day, the caravan stopped at a cluster of thorn trees and the company flopped under their stingy shade. Dogs panted, the horse's bridles chinked as they drank from leather water pails, the camels snorted at dry blades of sedge. Mustaar brought him some strips of cactus, wet and sweet, which Zadab slipped under the *bandeem*, his eyes never leaving the trail of their footprints that stretched to the far, flat horizon.

"No one follows," Mustaar murmured. Zadab knew better than to speak.

They rode again when the sun angled closer to the sands, stopping in the night at the next caravanserai. Mustaar unburdened the beast, shouldering Zadab aside when he attempted to help. In the privacy of their sleeping stall, they investigated Master Chaleem's bag, Mustaar muttering hopefully for treasure of some kind, rare spices or gems he was sure a nobleman would carry. Disappointingly, beside the desert traveler's kit of blanket and rug, kettle and cup, there were only a few brightly colored silk robes.

Mustaar squatted back on his haunches in disgust, but Zadab's fingers probed the bag, feeling their way to the false bottom as though they had known it was there. Beneath, were thick black robes wrapped around the leather book Mustaar had spoken of.

"Mage robes," Mustaar hissed, and sat eyeing this discovery like it was an unwanted guest at a feast. Finally, with the delicacy of a drover plucking a coal from a fire, he picked up the leather book. Neither of them could read, but someone with a mage's torque would likely have a book of spells, Zadab thought. "You shouldn't touch that," he cautioned, but a folded sheet of paper had already escaped from between the pages.

Zadab could see it was a map. The camel drovers didn't use maps, knowing the desert like they knew their own children. But he had seen merchants study such papers over the fires, sharing stories of the hazards painted there or of the markets ripe for profit.

He could make no sense of the markings, but Mustaar squinted at them, trailing a finger along the dotted lines.

Finally, he said, "I think this star is for Ashala's Folly and the pointed shapes along it are supposed to be the mountains of the Noose."

"So small!" Zadab marveled.

Mustaar snickered. "Those mountains are huge, I've heard. The very clouds make way for them. Master Chaleem talked about them like a man possessed." He shook his head. "He told me about a valley at the top of the world where there was some essence in the air, or the water, that would expand his abilities tenfold. But then he shouted at me to stop spying on him." He shook his head at the strange ways of the nobles.

An impulse Zadab couldn't understand drove him to snatch the paper from Mustaar's fingers. He heard himself say, "Keep it with the book." He had the oddest thought that if Mustaar possessed the map, he would possess something that was Zadab's own. Such a strange thought. Zadab had never owned anything. Even so, he tucked the map inside the leather cover and pushed the book back under the false bottom of the bag.

He folded the mage's robe into a cushion for his head and slept more soundly than he would have thought possible. Before the first cock crowed, he was awake, and Mustaar served him hot spiced tea with flat bread and honey. First thing in the morning! Zadab had never broken the fast before his labors. To eat without the pain of hunger was to be a wealthy man.

Once dressed in Master Chaleem's uncomfortable silks, he stepped out of the sleeping stall and stretched to his full height. A pair of drovers bowed their heads to him, and his chest puffed with importance.

Mustaar snorted. "They bow to the silks," he muttered, "not the man."

Zadab ignored him. He felt wonderful.

At midday, when Mustaar spilled tea onto the yellow silk of his robe, Zadab snapped at him. The lad's hands shook as he pressed a rag to the stain. "You sound like Master Chaleem." He darted a narrow-eyed glance at Zadab's *bandeem.* "The same words. Even your voice with that foreign way of speaking."

Zadab didn't answer. How could his own voice sound different? He was Zadab. He knew no other way of speaking. But this thought was chased by another that whispered inside his head. *No, that name is no longer yours.* He shivered. How could a voice in his head rob him of his name?

By evening, the caravan had toiled up into the high plateau, the last leg of its journey. Zadab shivered thorough the night in the cooler air, and it occurred to him to wear the mage's thick robes on the morrow. When he told Mustaar, the boy grew frantic. "What will the others in the caravan think if a mage appears suddenly among them? They know you as Master Chaleem. You must remain Master Chaleem until we reach Ashala's Folly."

Zadab did not care to have his slave telling him what to do. For a moment, he thought he might— His blinked in confusion. Whatever he thought he might do had faded like morning fog kissed by the sun. Instead, a kind of laughing emptiness filled his head and sent fingers of fear trailing down his spine.

He pulled on the robes in defiance, saying, "Then I will wear these beneath the nobleman's gaudy silks. No one will see the difference, just as they never noticed I was not Master Chaleem."

How amusing, a mage pretending to be a nobleman pretending to be a slave pretending to be a nobleman. Zadab frowned at the peculiar riddle that had flitted through his head. What had made him think such a thing? Was it not the other way around? He was a slave pretending to be a nobleman who— Again, his thoughts stuttered. He didn't know why the nobleman carried the garb of a mage. His head felt like a sack, the contents tossed about by thieves.

The camels moved faster over the firm ground of the plateau and Ashala's Folly rose into view. The mountains of the Noose nearly cleaved the sky, as Mustaar had told him, rearing up behind the fortress with its apron of markets and inns and bathhouses. Zadab had never seen a city before, but it was the Noose he couldn't tear his eyes from, those high, white-topped peaks, like so many blades thrust from the ground. *Finally,* he thought, *my destination.*

"That's where Master Chaleem was bound." Mustaar jutted his chin toward the range.

Zadab stared down at the lad until he realized his error and said swiftly, "I mean, *your* destination, Master Chaleem."

"That's better." Seeing the lad's discomfort was quite satisfying, but there was still something wrong. Zadab tipped his head, listening for the error. *Not Master Chaleem. That is not my name.* "You must call me Alsandor," he told Mustaar, and then wondered where that name had come from.

Mustaar looked to be having the same thought, but the gates of the city were opening, drawing their attention forward. Zadab wished he could cast aside the *bandeem* to better see the wonders of the crowded streets where tangles of people shuttled to and fro, shouting and toting baskets and clay jars and copper urns. Women stood on street corners beside heaping trays of fruits or vegetables, calling out their wares in singsong. Donkeys brayed outside of buildings, and children called from the windows to the travelers.

The noise and confusion were dizzying. He wanted to curl in upon himself and hide. *I am just Zadab, the water slave,* he thought, *not one for such splendor as this city.* Several young women in an upper balcony pointed and giggled in musical trills. *They are laughing at me. They can see I am not who I pretend to be.* Shame burned its way through him.

Stop playing the fool! The command felt like a slap in the face. Zadab jolted upright, pivoting his head to find the speaker. There was no one, but the voice didn't stop. *Turn at the street ahead and make for the Two Trees Serai.* Out of confusion more than anything else, Zadab obeyed.

Mustaar's protests followed him down the roadway. "Master Chaleem! Master Chaleem! Alsandor!" Then finally, dangerously, "Zadab!"

Zadab ignored him. A sign bearing the inscription *Two Trees Serai,* beckoned with its elegant gold script. "We stay here." He tossed the reins to Mustaar, adding, "Return the camels to the caravan and then wait for me in the stable." The boy's indignation and confusion nipped off as the door clapped shut behind him.

He instructed the slave squatting just inside to bring his bags and then paid for a room. *This is better,* he thought as he was shown into a private room with a proper bed and washstand and shutters drawn to block the city noise. He tore off the *bandeem* and sighed in relief.

When he bent over the wash bowl, the face that looked back from its still surface startled him. So young! His skin, the color of hammered bronze, was so smooth. But his eyes were like the dead of night. It was all wrong. As he stared at them, they grew lighter, becoming like the purple glow before dawn before brightening into the blue of morning. *Much better*, Alsandor thought.

The serai slave silently dropped the bags inside the doorway, gave him a startled look, and scuttled away, bowed at the waist with the subservience Alsandor found so demeaning. *No pride at all. How can they expect to be treated as men?*

But he had work to do. He discarded the gaudy silks he'd been forced to wear in his disguise as the imaginary nobleman he'd called Master Chaleem. Yes, he was feeling much better now.

For a while, he perused the notes he'd made in his journal before his unexpected death. By his own reckoning, he was surely the greatest living mage, but he had not foreseen his own premature demise in those tunnels. His mind had been otherwise occupied with his study of the springways. He had been sure that the waters from the mountains of the Noose, running untainted beneath the desert sands, would contain traces of the mystical essence reputed to fully liberate the powers of his mind. It had been exceptionally bad luck his heart had given out just then.

He'd been more than fortunate Mistress Sarroway had thought to send those two creatures looking for him. The slow-witted stupidity of the larger of the two had practically invited Alsandor's spirit to slip in unchallenged. Zadab's strong, young body was a decided improvement from his own, which had suffered the pains of a life lived too long and unwisely.

It would be a fine body to keep, he thought. Were he able to obtain the essence he sought, no longer would he be forced to suffer the indignities of an aging body, let alone death. He could keep this one young almost indefinitely. If a man were able to pat himself on the back, Alsandor would have done so. Instead, he only smiled inwardly, accepting his own congratulations. *Yes, things were looking up all considered.*

A faint noise disturbed his thoughts, like the mewling of a kitten. The water slave was making pitiful attempts to regain his own voice. It would be a losing battle. Alsandor had sequestered that feeble spirit so deep inside his mind, it would never find his way to the surface.

It had taken years for Alsandor to achieve such mastery over the transcendent rivers of energy that wove through the world. And what had the mages done? Condemned him! Censured him! Forced him to flee into this superstitious, foreign land.

Well, he'd have the last laugh. Wearing the disguise of Master Chaleem, he'd turned his disgrace to advantage at the Zandimyn gaming tables. His skills had won him the map, a prize of unimaginable value charting the way to the legendary land he sought, where the essence mysterious essence grew. Its discovery would be the crowning achievement of his life.

As they'd drawn closer to the Noose, he'd felt the pull of that land as a hunger within him. This next leg of the journey, though, would require preparations. He'd have Mustaar hire horses and a guide. He rose, steadying himself on the washstand. His strength had not yet recovered from the ordeal of his death and his usurpation of the mind and body of another. Fatigue ate at his very bones. On top of that, controlling the mindless gibbering of the water slave in his head was giving him a headache.

Perhaps the constant pain of his pinched feet was affecting him. How Zadab had walked about on such great flapping paddles he had no idea. He hobbled down to the stables where he found Mustaar sulking sullen-eyed among the other beasts of burden.

Before he could get a word in, the lad leapt up, berating him in frightened whispers. "Zadab! What are you doing? You shouldn't be wearing the mage robe in public. Nor the torque! No good will come of that." The lad was near to tearing out his hair in his anxiety.

He stopped suddenly in front of the man he took to be Zadab. "And what do you mean by staying in this place? We can't afford it!"

"It is a bit on the dear side," Alsandor said.

Open-mouthed, Mustaar stared straight into Alsandor's face before falling back with a sharp cry. "Your eyes! They are as the daytime sky. What magic is this?" He spat to the side and then drew breath to shout his alarm.

Mustaar was cleverer than Alsandor had anticipated. His quick wits had revealed themselves when he'd thought to rob Alsandor's corpse, which even he had to admit showed spirit. But now the boy understood things were not as they seemed. A shame.

He drew on his fading reserves of strength to pluck the threads of the world, murmured softly, and caught the lad's voice as it began to pour from his body. He bound it and stored it safely, while the boy, hearing the silence of his own shouts, staggered into the straw, clutching his throat.

What have you done to my friend? The voice in Alsandor's head sounded like it came from a great distance. He sneered at it. *Your 'friend' is a good deal more clever than you, lad. He kept all the coin in Master Chaleem's purse and you never even noticed. I had to steal it back while you slept. Half-wit.*

Mustaar was flailing as though in his death throes. He would do himself an injury if he kept this up, Alsandor thought. Annoyed, he gripped the lad's arm and pulled him to his feet. Mustaar's mouth flexed uselessly, his eyes knotting in pain.

Stop hurting him! Zadab's words were startlingly clear in his head.

I've simply put his voice elsewhere for safekeeping, Alsandor told the slow-witted prisoner. *He can have it back when it's more convenient for me.*

Why was he explaining himself? He shook his head and focused on the thrashing slave in his hand. Well, what had been an expense on one end of the trip, would turn a profit on the other.

As he dragged Mustaar through the congested alleys, the half-wit in his head shouted that he, Zadab, had been a slave. Alsandor hardly needed any reminding. The indignity of it had inflamed him like an infestation of sand fleas.

The robe makes the man, he told his beast of burden. *I wear the robes now, and I chose to sell an inconvenient slave.* Though it would be pleasant to silence the irritating voice permanently, Alsandor wasn't sure he could destroy Zadab's dim spirit outright without causing harm to the body he now wore. His secret study had not anticipated such a thing. Nor was it a risk he could take so close to his destination.

And that destination was calling to him. If only his head didn't feel as pinched as his tortured toes. He squeezed his eyes to still the pain and suddenly realized his prisoner was no longer in his thoughts. It was as if a candle had been snuffed out, leaving only silence. He breathed in relief. It seemed the lad had saved him the trouble of having to kill him. Lack of will, is what it was, he thought. Men who are enslaved lack spine. They are so easily cowed.

The slave market was in full swing, the cool of evening bringing a fresh burst of business. Alsandor thrust Mustaar at the first green-belted slaver he encountered. Mustaar's temporary muteness devalued him, but Alsandor no longer cared. He was eager to turn his back on the betrayal painted on Mustaar's stricken face, and his fingers trembled slightly as he accepted too few silvers in exchange. Unaccountably, he felt soiled, and found himself wishing for nothing more than to escape the noise of the market and the terrified gaze of the slave.

It was clear he had been more weakened by his death than he had anticipated. He needed rest before attempting the journey into the mountains. In the peace of his private room at the *Two Trees Serai,* he didn't even disrobe before tumbling quickly into the oblivion of unconsciousness.

Most of him did.

A part of him was still quite conscious. It was comfortable being in the dark, and it was patient. It bided its time in the deep well of the mage's mind until the small hours of morning when it was accustomed to rising to start the waterwheel. And so, long before the first cock crow, Zadab climbed silently out of the darkness and took back control of his body, cautiously testing that his arms and legs moved at his own command.

'The robes make the man' the mage had told him. In that case, Zadab thought, to disrobe the man was to unmake the man. He fumbled with the buttons of the mage's robe and let it pool at his feel like an oily puddle. He felt stronger just stepping free of it. His hand hesitated over the torque at his neck. A thought surfaced that if he removed the torque just yet, the slumbering mage would surely sense its loss and awaken. Instead, he slipped a silken scarf beneath it and was rewarded by an easing of some weight inside his mind. It felt a bit like when he'd removed Master Chaleem's *bandeem*. Like he could breathe again.

He stowed Alsandor's gear into Master Chaleem's bag. To unmake the man, these would need to be destroyed. For now, he would slip out in the streets in the robes of Master Chaleem.

Luck guided him past a narrow alley where laundry hung on lines stretched from building to building. Among the rags, small clothes, women's skirts, and servants' tunics, he spotted a plain blue robe the color of water when the sun sits upon it. Such a robe, he thought, that would tell the world that he, Zadab, was a free man.

Swiftly, he flicked it from the line, leaving Master Chaleem's silks in its stead. To steal the robe was wrong, he knew, a poor way to buy his freedom, but perhaps its owner would find the exchange fair.

Wearing the blue robe felt like being wrapped in a piece of the sky, and he smiled for the first time in days. He pocketed the coin purse that had been so fattened by the sale of Mustaar and plucked up the bag with the mage's things. Above the tops of the buildings, he'd seen the smudge of smoke rising from the edge of the city. Smoke meant fire, and fire destroyed.

He stepped back out into the street. A slave in his earthen colored tunic scuttled to the side, head bowed. He bows to the clothes, Zadab thought, not the man. He straightened, more to be the man his clothes made others believe he was. A free man.

But he would need to hurry. As long as Alsandor lived within him, his body would be slave to the mage's greater power, regardless of his robes. Worse, he'd learned enough of the mage's mind to understand the essence he sought in the mountains could grant him such great power, he might keep the body he had stolen for uncountable years. Zadab would become a prisoner in his own body for uncountable years. It was unimaginable horror.

His focus slipped at the thought, and in that moment, something within him stirred like a black wave in the springways coming hard and fast. He began to run toward the edge of the city where the rubbish middens burned. Without hesitation, he pitched the bag with the mage's robes into the fires and watched as it began to smolder. As he reached to unclasp the torque from his neck, the bag burst into flames which danced like sunset unleashed upon the middens. He gaped in wonder.

Then Alsandor awoke.

Fool! Fool! Fool! The voice slammed into Zadab's head like blows from a blacksmith's hammer. His fingers froze on the torque, refusing his will.

He was too late.

He began to run in blind panic, listening only to the familiar sound of his bare feet slapping the stones of the street. He ran until Alsandor's greater will clamped his legs still. He stood gasping for air and realized he was at the foot of the steep mountain road. The breath of the high range flowed down it, cold and clean. Alsandor saw it as well.

Zadab felt the mage's craving growing with each breath of that sweet mountain air. The craving was far greater than any desire Zadab had ever felt for a friend, for a full belly, or even for freedom. Power unspeakable lay somewhere in those high peaks and filled the mage's thoughts until they wept the excess of it.

He felt himself wallowing in the vastness of Alsandor's desire and then his body was goaded up the mountain road, into the heights that led to the source of that power. As they climbed, the mage began to laugh.

There had been a mad man once at the caravanserai who had laughed in the same way, Zadab remembered. He'd stare at the moon and laugh without restraint, without caution. Eventually, he'd run into the desert and died under the eye of the sun.

Hiding from the raving of the mage in his own head, Zadab knew that Alsandor was quite mad. He would run his beast of burden until Zadab died of exhaustion.

Yet still he ran at the mage's bidding, barely aware he climbed above the rooftops of the city, above the walls of the old fortress that guarded it, above the line of trees, above the hawks who carved the blue sky with their wings.

By the time he reached the crest of the ridge, his lungs felt flayed and his throat was a dry gully. On both sides of the knife-edge upon which he stood, the world fell away from him. To the south, Ashala's Folly seemed a scattering of children's blocks left out in the morning sun. To the north, the land fell away into a deep ravine before jutting up again like knives from the heart of the world.

He teetered there, staring into the emptiness beneath his feet, his splayed toes gripping the jagged rock. It was a long way down. It would be a very long fall. Zadab felt the rising panic in Alsandor's mind as the mage also stared into that yawning void, knowing its strange pull.

Yes, Zadab shouted to the mage, *we will fall a long, long way.*

Alsandor's mind recoiled, scrabbling senselessly back into the recesses of Zadab's mind. In that moment, Zadab was released. He tore the copper torque from his neck and hurled it as far as he could. It rose, singing as it spun away over the treetops before slicing a path deep into the ravine. As it fell, Zadab heard another cry, a lunatic song of fear and desire that faded into a sigh of pain. It came from everywhere and nowhere at the same time and finally faded into echoes that sounded like *No- no -no* in Zadab's thoughts.

He stood with head bowed for a while, listening. He could still hear Alsandor within him, but it was a broken sound, like a clay vessel endlessly shattering until finally he heard nothing at all.

A hawk screamed in passing. He lifted his head and watched it cut the air and grow smaller over the highest peaks of the Noose where an essence could be found that would give a man great power. Zadab had never had any power. Alsandor had had too much. He watched the hawk disappear into a sky the color of his robe.

Then he snorted and turned back down the mountain path at a light trot, the coin purse jingling in the pocket of his blue robe. He had something more important to do.

This is the final issue of The Fifth Di... To those who have contributed to this publication and/or read it, we thank you for your participation. The Fifth Di... was originally created by the late James B. Baker in 1998, went into print in 2008, and so has been around for 26 years—a lifetime in the world of the small indie presses.

We hope you will continue to check out our site at <u>www.hiraethsffh.com</u>, buy our books (yes, and read them ▢ ▢ and tell others about us.

Bon voyage...